Beck did the only other thing he could think of: he wrapped his arms around her and tugged enough to get her that last step to him.

Lauren froze, stiff as an oak in his arms, and possibly stopped breathing except she whispered, "You're hugging me…"

"Yeah…" He tilted his head to the side as she tilted hers up, dirty, pink, exhausted, and in that second, devoid of all the awful emotions that had been written in capital letters on her face. "You should be warned, I'm also kind of thinking of kissing you. But that would probably be a bad idea."

Bad, and not something he did anymore. He just preferred to live his life on his own, free of the mess that came with relationships. His celibacy had even become easy at this point. And yet, with this woman, he wanted to forget all the reasons it was a bad idea to get more involved.

RESCUED BY
HER RIVAL

———

AMALIE BERLIN

⟨H⟩ **HARLEQUIN**® MEDICAL ROMANCE™

Recycling programs
for this product may
not exist in your area.

ISBN-13: 978-1-335-64157-1

Rescued by Her Rival

First North American Publication 2019

Copyright © 2019 by Amalie Berlin

Printed in U.S.A.

Visit the Author Profile page
at Harlequin.com for more titles.

CHAPTER ONE

FIREFIGHTER AND SMOKEJUMPER trainee Lauren Autry jogged with the rest of the herd to the large field behind the main hall at the old twentieth-century 4-H camp the Forest Service had repurposed for spring training facilities.

Every year since the nineteen-fifties new recruits and veteran smokejumpers alike descended upon a handful of camps littering the Northwestern United States for the intense training required to prepare them for the coming wildfire season. The elite firefighting service only took the fittest, the most capable of conquering and surviving the remote, treacherous terrain where wildfires tended to explode—parachuting in with simple tools and supplies to fight and contain big, dangerous blazes, only to be rewarded with a long hike back to civilization after the job was done.

Only the best made it through, and if Lauren had been lacking two years ago, she'd made up for it since then, throwing herself into every kind of study and training she could conceive of—even things not required, at least when her job and family responsibilities hadn't gotten in the way. She'd trained harder, pushed herself beyond her already insane standards. If only she could've figured out how to grow a few more inches, everything would be perfect. And if she'd gotten to complete the civilian skydiving course she'd been counting on. That was something she should've better controlled. Better planned for. Not required, she'd get to learn it here, but still. Prepared. Making up for any deficiencies. That had been the plan.

If she made it to a crew—*when* she made it to a crew—no one would be able to question whether she was capable. Whether she was tall enough, or strong enough, or *good* enough. Never again. Not her brothers. Not her father. None of the hundreds of dead ancestors who'd been serving the same San Francisco fire station since its founding in the nineteenth century…not that she could hear *their* critiques, at least.

No more of those questions she'd been suffering the six years since she'd become a firefighter. No more of the insinuations her failure two years ago had amplified.

No more holding pattern of derailed life plans.

This year she'd made it through the selection process, even under the authority of Chief

Treadwell, the same man who'd passed her over before and given the last spot to a no-neck marine.

None of that mattered. She was here *now*.

This was really happening!

The thought sent a jittery, tingling wave washing over her scalp again, every cell in her body seeming to light up at once. It had taken every ounce of willpower to sit still and pay attention through orientation, before she began the endurance test she'd been primed for two years to run. The simple act of moving again, letting her body do what it had been conditioned to do, was the kind of physical relief she'd like to also have mentally.

The crowd stopped in the grass, and so did she, but behind a sea of broad shoulders and crewcuts, she couldn't see what was going on.

Right. Identify the problem, find the solution.

Turning sideways, she slipped and ducked through the crowd to reach the front, and the unexciting view of three older men with clipboards quietly conversing while everyone else waited. More waiting. More need to move crawling over her knees. An itch to get started. Prove herself. Prove to Treadwell he'd made a mistake passing her over for what's-his-face.

Soon enough, they began calling names and sorting those assembled into three different groups. When that was done, one look around confirmed: her group was peopled with rookies—she could tell by their yellow badges. All new people. All new *dudes*. And her. Which was fine. Expected, even. It was the smallest group, which was also fine. She'd get more attention that way. The right kind of attention. Training attention. Proving-herself attention.

Her group split off, moving to the side of the large dirt track to hear the rules again.

Endurance test, first. Mile and a half in under eleven minutes. Easy-peasy. She barely needed to stretch for that, but did anyway.

"Ellison!" Treadwell barked the name just as she'd caught one ankle behind her to stretch her quads, causing her to pitch to the side then scramble to stay upright.

"You're late!"

Chief. Shouting.

Someone late the first day?

Ellison.

The name caught up with her and she jolted again.

Beck Ellison. Her nemesis! Who likely had no idea he was her nemesis… The Golden Boy she'd only quasi creeped on online because when a girl had a secret nemesis… Well, social media was far too easy to peek at. Not that she'd been hoping to see anything bad. In fact, she hadn't seen anything at all in terms of a profile for the man. She'd just seen posts *about* him doing this and that, articles in different newspapers used as PR for the service. Stuff she couldn't help but see and feel the knife twisting in her spleen every time he did something else wonderful. *Smoke Charmer nonsense.*

She could do her job without an ego-stoking nickname.

Smoke Charmer.

Then again, if she had to lose out to someone, better he be astounding than abysmal. If she *had* to lose.

Positive thoughts. Positive thoughts. Maintain habit of sending good intentions out to the universe.

Maybe he was there to teach them all how to become one with the fire, *Smoke Charmer* style.

She turned slightly from her position at the starting line to catch sight of a tall, shaggy-haired man jogging onto the track to join the group. Curls. That was new. The man had shiny black curls, wafting on the breeze as he jogged to the track—the only trace she could see of his past life as a marine was his fitness. Also new? He had a neck now.

And he was coming to run. Not there to teach. There to run. With the rookies.

His badge was yellow.

Rookie yellow.

He was being placed with the rookies?

Not again. He'd made it two years ago. He didn't need to weasel into her group now and start showing off.

She took a breath and got back in position at the track. In through the nose, out through the mouth.

This wasn't a competition. Not one that he *knew* about, at least. She just sort of…wanted to do better than he did. Today. And every day for the next six weeks.

"Did we inconvenience your plans to sleep in?" Treadwell barked, but Ellison—or the beefy, bipedal sheepdog now impersonating the formerly chisel-cut marine—didn't respond. He just dropped something black and plastic beside the track and got himself ready to run.

With. The. Rookies.

Let it go. Let it go and focus. She could tumble down some kind of rookie revirginization rabbit hole later, after she smoked him on the track. His legs might be longer, but hers would be *faster*.

The chief blew a whistle and she launched forward. All the anxious energy that had made her squirm in her seat through the arduous sixty-three-minute orientation finally freed.

She ran, everything falling into place as she pounded down the dirt track, her sneakers giving only the slightest slide on the hard-packed earth and gravel as she flew down the center lane. The heavy feeling of worry she'd been carrying with her for days suddenly lifted.

She'd always been a runner. The intense conditioning she'd put herself through was built on a lifetime of running, ever since she'd started T-ball and soccer, because her brothers had all played and they hadn't taken it easy on her, even at six.

Doing what she was meant to do, made her strong. With the track underfoot, she felt peace. She felt in control of her destiny. Able to overcome that small mistake she'd made on her application...

In a matter of seconds, the group she'd started with thinned. Sixteen started at her heels, and before her lungs even began to burn, she no longer heard feet pounding beside her. Or behind her. Even when listening hard.

Nope. No one. She was alone.

Which was when she remembered: *this wasn't a race.* She wasn't supposed to be outrunning anyone. Not even Ellison. She was supposed to be *outlasting* them. This was an endurance test. And speed ate up endurance. Endurance she'd need to make it through the day.

It took some effort to slow herself down, she felt it every clap of her heels against the packed earth, jarring her bones.

Six laps was the expected minimum. She'd go longer just to show she could. Not faster. Longer. Longer than them. Longer than Ellison.

She made it to the third lap before she gave in to temptation to look behind her. The closest to her, who seemed to be moving at a much steadier lope? Ellison. Of course, he was taller. Longer legs didn't need to run as hard for the same speed.

Never mind.

By the fourth lap her lungs were pretty warm.

By the sixth she legit wanted to stop. She could still finish first, but she wanted to finish *best.*

By the seventh lap, he'd caught up to her and when she gave in to the temptation to look up at him, she was met with one arched brow that said three things.

I know you.

I remember how competitive you were last time.

I still think you're an idiot.

For the briefest second, her vision swam with a lovely little brain movie of her throwing one leg to one side and sending his curly arrogance into the dirt. But then her vision cleared, and the sweeter side of her nature took over. She looked back to the track, and kept running.

Eight.

When was he going to stop? Were they actually racing now? Was this a thing that was happening?

Other people had already stopped.

Eight and a half… Treadwell whistled again, loud and shrill. A call to stop. She let inertia carry her forward a few more yards to slow and stop naturally.

Hands on her knees, she kept herself up and gulped air, sweat plastering her shirt to her back, and the grit she'd kicked up from the dirt track rubbing like sandpaper against her bare legs. Should've stopped after the seventh.

"Not a race, Autry." Ellison panted too, where he'd stopped a couple lanes away, the curls she hated to admire a little crisper from the light sweat he'd built.

Of course he'd have better hair too.

And not the point. Not a race, he'd said, but he'd still kept up with her ridiculous pace.

"Tell yourself."

She straightened, less inclined to bear the grudging respect she'd built for him since he'd turned out to actually be something special, someone she could feel better about herself for having lost to, and walked much more slowly to center field, where the chief gathered his group again.

Ignore Ellison. What was next?

Maybe water. Please, let there be water.

* * *

Beck followed Autry off the track, his breathing more rapid than his sluggish thoughts. He'd been in a haze all week, trying to decide what his life was supposed to be, and had quietly hoped that once he'd made his decision the fog would lift, and he'd know whether he still had it in him to be what he'd felt called to his whole life.

No such luck. The only thing clear was his broken life compass. And that he'd somehow annoyed the woman he'd briefly met two years prior.

She seemed fit. Maybe a little harder than she had been. Normally, he'd say harder was a good thing—harder emotions meant distance, control, better decision-making in dangerous situations. But annoyed was just another flavor of the same emotional unsteadiness he'd seen in her when she'd gone teary after not making the ranks.

She'd sworn to Treadwell she'd be back next year. Last year. Was that another fail? Surprising, but probably no more than it was for her to see him as a rookie this year too.

Didn't matter. Once training was complete, she'd be off to her own unit and her emotionalism wouldn't be his problem. He had his own issues to focus on.

Before joining the others, he stopped to retrieve the radio he'd dropped earlier and wedged one earbud in to get another update on the wild-fire he'd been monitoring since yesterday. A dry winter and an even drier spring meant the fire season had come early. When rain and runoff existed, spring wildfires were easier to handle and didn't grow at the vicious speed this one was. The team would be called in today, for sure. If luck was with him, the call would come before he'd spent himself on the rookie field, while he still had enough energy to give Treadwell a reason to stop looking at him like he was the embodiment of all human disappointment.

The radio crackled and he stopped en route to the coolers, but no report followed. Maybe luck wouldn't be with him. It certainly hadn't been with him last season.

He grabbed a drink and joined the others, half listening to Treadwell go over the next exercise, the other tuned into the earpiece. It was the first day, and his attention was rightly divided. He didn't need to hear the physical requirements, he remembered them. Listening for the call was an act of team spirit, for his true team. Not these rookies. Besides, no one was a spirited teammate on day one. Team-building took more than a day.

He worked better alone anyway—fewer distractions. Fewer *people* to worry about. Something that hadn't been a problem until last season.

One mistake had turned the chief's opinion of him upside down.

Turned him upside down too. Getting back out there today would help in a way that four months tending his forest territory had somehow failed to help.

If his chief didn't also take the rookies every year, he might not have even had the opportunity to try again, and he wasn't ready to picture a future where this wasn't his job. That meant he had to show up, do whatever Treadwell demanded for the next several weeks. Wear his rookie badge. Take his lumps.

Be like Autry.

She stood so straight and stiff she might as well have been in a muster, her attention narrowed on the chief with laser precision. Though none of what he said could've been news to her, the physical requirements were public information. Requirements that included the height minimum, so she'd certainly have read them.

As if feeling his gaze, she turned his direction, and met his steady examination with folded arms and a churlish bent to her brows. Still annoyed.

Whatever. He looked back at the radio because of another round of crackling static, and the next he knew, she was at his side.

"They stuck you with the new recruits?"

Her breathing had already leveled out, the only

evidence of her prior exertion the pinkness of her cheeks. She'd run as if chased by wolves, but looked none the worse for wear. He should probably ask what had happened to last year, but that would only encourage conversation. And questions in return.

"Looks like it," he muttered, and turned up the volume on the single earpiece as a quick buzz announced an incoming report.

"What are you listening to?"

"Reports."

"Reports on what?"

He narrowed his eyes at the middle distance, feigning concentration, and pressed the earpiece into his ear, glad for a reason to tune out.

Not glad there was such a monstrous fire so early in the season, but he wanted to get at it. He was still on the team. If Treadwell went, he'd go too. His yellow badge was penance.

She finally took his silence for the hint it was and stopped prodding him for answers. There were plenty of other people to pester, and she didn't know the report had long since ended and now he pretended to listen to dead air.

Treadwell began calling names again, dividing his group into three, and Beck found himself sorted to the bar, along with Autry, who was now busy introducing herself to the others in their team, making friends. Smiling. Showing her team spirit.

"Ellison's not new," he heard her say, calling his attention back to the newly formed subgroup. "He made it a couple years ago. But…uh… I guess he got stuck with us because he was late."

Wrong.

"This is Alvarez, Finnegan, and Wyler."

Still talking to him. No longer annoyed. She actually looked excited, a brightness in her eyes out of step with what was actually happening. Push-ups. Pull-ups. Sit-ups… Not exactly a party.

Treadwell called his name, saving him from making nice, and he stepped to the bar, pausing only long enough to deposit his radio on the ground and free his hands. The chief's gaze wordlessly followed him and Beck said two words before reaching for the bar to pull himself up. "It's bigger."

A frown and a nod were his only acknowledgments, and Treadwell began to count as Beck got on with it. As soon as he'd passed the minimum number of pull-ups, he dropped down for sit-ups, then rolled to push-ups, stopping each time he'd passed the required amount, leaving himself room to "improve" as camp continued.

Treadwell's arched brow? Beck shrugged a touch. "Conserving energy."

His muscles buzzing, he pulled himself off the

ground, retrieved his radio, then went for another drink so he could sit on the grass to watch the others work their way through as he listened.

Still no new reports to free him.

Autry had been in the middle of the five, but as he watched, she talked herself to the rear of the group.

She'd learn soon enough how to survive these days: go early, get it over with, don't waste energy showing off. Take all opportunities to rest.

Or not. Maybe it was better for *him* if she kept doing whatever she was doing. If she finished too soon, she'd be there beside him, asking questions. Making a nuisance of herself with her newbie enthusiasm.

CHAPTER TWO

THE INSTANT THE call for more crews came over the radio, Beck sprang to his feet.

Finally. Time to get out of this. He headed for Treadwell, who stood with clipboard in hand, counting the reps of another rookie.

The chatter he'd expect from Autry had never come when she'd gotten done with her turn at the bar. Treadwell had stopped her from showing off by making her finish her reps when it became clear she had no idea what a reasonable number was. She'd been sitting on the grass, sulking, ever since, her formerly animated brow becoming a little ledge above her pretty green eyes.

Pretty?

He mentally shook himself. They were striking, an evergreen ring around a pale center. If anything, they were unusual and therefore compelling. Him fixating on eye color meant he needed to get out of there. Had spent too much time alone in the woods, lost in his own head.

Then again, no one lurked in the forest to constantly remind him of this nonsense about him undoing core tenets of his personality over a few short weeks. People went to years of therapy to change habits and outlooks acquired over a lifetime, and he had no interest in that either.

"Chief." He interrupted the rookie doing push-ups with one word and a meaningful waggle of his radio, indicating the call had come.

Treadwell's gaze narrowed and he nodded, but held up one hand in Beck's direction and told the man on the ground he could stop.

He and Treadwell might not be on the same page on everything, but over the past two years the man had learned to interpret Beck's admittedly spartan method of communication. Beck liked him for that. Liked him in general, really.

During his first year, back when it'd seemed he could do no wrong, he'd still had to actively work to be something like what they expected off duty. They'd accepted his tendency to go off on his own when he got a whiff of something during a fire. Let him come around to telling them whatever he'd concluded when he was certain.

He didn't know where that sixth sense had gone, could only hope it had come back over the winter. Knowing how far he'd fallen in the chief's esteem chafed.

After marking the rookie's reps and still carrying his clipboard, Treadwell strode in Beck's direction. The stout man was in his fifties, and probably as fit as when he'd joined. "What's the call?"

"Us and two other units." Beck nodded down the field to where the other groups were breaking up. "About a forty-five-minute flight. Kolinski said he'd pack our gear and hold the plane."

Treadwell listened and nodded, but just when Beck thought he was going to turn around and give the grunts the afternoon off he said, "Not you."

"It's a big fire. You need me."

"Not like this I don't."

The urge to argue burned his throat, but he clamped his teeth together. Not that he didn't buck orders on occasion, but only when he had some measure of certainty he was right to do so. He wanted to argue that no one in the unit read fires like he did, but he simply wasn't sure that was the case any longer. That was last year's argument. Before his mistakes. Before he'd been trapped by the flames.

Treadwell handed him the clipboard. Accepting the transfer of the hard acrylic gave him a sensation somewhat like the first time he'd jumped from a plane. Plummeting. Ground that approached far too rapidly.

He stood straighter. Even without that one selling point, he was still as capable as anyone else. "You're sure? I'm still boots on the ground."

"Your boots are on whatever ground you see fit. This is the first day. Prove me wrong and we'll talk."

He wanted to, if he actually knew how to follow orders he knew were wrong. As annoying as the yellow badge might be, at least probation gave him more time to sort things out.

When Beck said nothing else, the chief turned to summon Autry with a wave.

She'd been watching—everyone in the group had been—and at the summons she popped out of her sulk and trotted right over.

"You two finish morning PT with the group," Treadwell said, adding, "There's a fire, and Ellison has already expended too much energy to give one hundred percent this morning, he doesn't need to throw himself into the blaze at less than full capacity."

Yes, he did. He needed that.

"I'm fine," he argued finally, the prospect of minding rookies worse than simply sitting out a fight.

Treadwell shot him a hard look, one that Beck could also interpret. Punishment or probation, it didn't matter, he was out of the game until this was done, and Treadwell was trying to save face on his behalf.

Beck would've gladly taken the ding to his pride if it would've gotten him back into the fray. Sitting around with a clipboard while his team jumped into danger didn't sit right.

Treadwell thumped him on the shoulder once and before Autry could ask any of the questions bouncing around in those strange green eyes he finalized his orders. "Handle the rest of the baselines. Classroom was going to be protocols, but since it looks like most of us will be in the field, Ellison's going to do a Q&A about service, lessons learned his first couple years. Then you can all amuse yourselves for the rest of the day, but be on the field at daybreak tomorrow before the siren blasts."

Autry still looked confused, but she nodded and had now shifted her attention to *him*, her expression saying things he didn't want to hear—like she got just how little he wanted to do this. "What do you want me to do?"

All of it.

Eager to get rid of the clipboard, he passed the cursed thing over and gestured for her to follow. The sooner they got on with it, the sooner he could get it over with.

"Three crews have been called to a blaze, Treadwell wants us to continue," he announced, straight to the point, then added, because it would help them to know the course when it became mandatory, "After that, lunch, and then a five-mile run around the woodland course."

Autry cleared her throat, and for a second he thought it was because she was going to correct him about the run, but instead she said, "Don't forget the classroom Q&A before the run."

One tiny twitch of an eyebrow challenged him to argue, but she didn't correct Treadwell's orders—probably because she was obsessive about exercise. Couldn't rightly fault her for it, except that she didn't let him get away with sidestepping the exercise in public speaking.

"Q&A after lunch. Five questions. Then run." He returned her look. In unison, her brows and shoulders popped up. She might as well have just said, *Whatever*.

Whatever. He got back to the task at hand, gesturing to the man Treadwell had been testing, still on the ground. "Who are you?"

"San Giovanni."

"He only has sit-ups left," Autry added.

He'd have been happy to let her continue on her own, but Treadwell's opinion wasn't going to be raised by his desire to maintain the ten-foot ring of *emptiness* around himself he preferred.

"How many are left after him?"

"Six."

He nodded once for the man to continue and silently counted while the man got on with it.

* * *

Lunch came and went, and Lauren found herself back on the field with the other rookies, waiting for Ellison.

He'd said about twenty words before lunch, and most of those had been numbers, or *Next*. He'd been chattier two years ago.

If saying more than one word per breath could ever be considered chatty. He only barely communicated at a level higher than grunts and too-easy-to-read judgmental faces. But he *had* communicated more last time. His current level of terseness seemed the type usually reserved for people who'd caused offense. Which couldn't be her.

Unless he thought she stank at everything and couldn't believe she'd returned for a second try? Wouldn't be the first time she'd encountered that. Or the thousandth.

Women weren't unheard of in the service, but they weren't abundant either. Even with her firefighting pedigree, the weight of the Autry name probably just meant people would expect her to be *better*. Not making it two years ago had contradicted that notion, even though she'd served her family's station since fresh from high school and her father had known better than to turn her away lest she go to a station where he couldn't control her. Then six years of hard-fought experience, and the arguments it had taken to get it.

She looked at her watch. Two more minutes and Ellison would be late. Probably because he didn't want to do the Q&A.

She could imagine now how it'd go.

What was the rating on the largest fire you encountered this year?

Big.

Where do you see yourself in five years?

Here.

What's your biggest weakness?

Talking.

When the hour struck one, and not a second before, Ellison jogged up from the food hall and onto the field. If someone's posture could shout belligerence, his did. He held himself so erect she'd have expected his collarbone to snap with an accidental shoulder twitch. Everyone else seemed to pick up on it too. Absorbed it so well even that when he asked for questions, no one said a word for a long time, until Lauren shot her hand up. To help him out, of course. Not just to torture him. To get the ball rolling. And because she wasn't scared of a grumpy off-season forest ranger.

"You've been at it two seasons. Have you had any close calls? Or, you know, back when you were a combat firefighter? That could be cool to hear about."

He shouldn't look so surprised, she'd only had *forever* to dwell on what had gone wrong last time. Marine combat firefighter? More impressive than the daughter of a local chief who only let her into the fires when she was able to outmaneuver him.

She wasn't outmaneuvering Ellison. He held his tongue long enough that it seemed like he was translating words in his head, and then produced a miserly portion to answer only the first part, ignoring her question about his surly marine firefighting days. Another hand went up and the conversation moved on.

Where was the biggest blaze?

Did he enjoy the off-season? What did he do?

Forest ranger. Clearing brush. Controlled burns.

Nailed it!

Biggest mistake people made in the field?

Most useful advice to someone starting out?

That last one was the one that tripped him up. His mouth opened and closed no fewer than three times, and she could all but see him sorting through his options of advice to dole out. It meant nothing to her if he had so much advice to give he couldn't decide on what was best, but when he spoke, he sounded like someone parrot-

ing words given to him at some point. Like he
didn't believe a word of what came out.

"Your team is your biggest asset. Be a team
player. Watch out for your team. Follow orders."

One look around confirmed that everyone
thought this advice was *basic*, but he cut the
questions off, having just scraped five, and sent
everyone for their woodland run.

Everyone but her, the one who'd actually heard
the chief's orders. She went to fetch her things
from the boot of her car, and on her way back
through, stopped beside where he sat on the
grass, hands behind him, propping himself up.

"Go Team, eh?"

He ignored her question again, his gaze fixed
across the field to the wooden steps that led up
to the rough, woodland running track where he'd
sent them. "Not running?"

"You forget, I actually heard what the chief
said." She grinned down at him, not that he was
looking, and put down her duffel. "I don't see
you running either."

"I will. When the crowd thins."

"So will I."

"They need to do it."

She hadn't questioned that. Of course, they
needed to do it. It was called Hell Week for a reason. Every one of them was supposed to come out
in better shape than they'd gone in, and no one

got better by sitting on their butt, enjoying the blistering afternoon sunshine, as he was doing. "No argument from me. I'm just getting my gear moved into a cabin first."

"Cabin assignments haven't been made yet."

Contrary creature. Looking for things to pick apart? Lent more weight to the notion that he just didn't want her there.

She could really tick him off by sitting down beside him, where he looked far too comfortable, his muscled legs sprawled out in the grass. The man wasn't bulky, but he was dense and lean in a way that made the shape of every muscle down his arms and legs show under hair-dusted skin.

He'd had a certain soldierly hunkiness before, but now he looked like he'd dulled all his sharp, military corners except for those of his physique. Longer hair. Loose cotton clothes. White and gray, no khaki or green anywhere. And he spent enough time in the woods that he wasn't as bronzed as he'd been either.

All softening touches. And somehow he was more churlish. Strange that years *after* leaving combat he'd become less friendly. By the look of him, and the way he'd stood apart from everyone, this man was the one who most needed a friend. What had he even been saying?

Oh, right. She was picking her own cabin, not waiting on orders. Blah-blah cabin shenanigans.

They would've made cabin assignments today if everyone hadn't been called to the field for an emergency.

"Do you really think the chief wouldn't want everyone having a bed?"

"They do things a particular way."

"And they can do things that way tomorrow." She shrugged, shifting topic. "What's your plan?"

"Truck." He looked up at her finally.

Back to one-word answers.

"Did you have a stutter as a child?"

"What? No."

"Propensity for mispronouncing words?"

"No."

"Do you have some kind of a Samson situation going on in reverse? The longer your hair gets, the weaker your vocabulary?"

"What are you talking about?"

"You were more talkative last time we met," she answered, "even if you weren't exactly Mr. Conversation. Did something bad happen that you find painful to revisit?"

He actually paled then and she immediately felt bad for asking. Suddenly it was something she couldn't joke about. Something bad *had* happened. And now he was a rookie.

No smokejumpers had died, she would've heard if there had been any deaths. They were so well trained and prepared they could go decades without a fatality.

"Nothing happened."

The man was not a good liar, at least not when directly questioned.

Lauren's friends were mostly men, due to the nature of her profession. She wasn't a native speaker of Dude Language, but she had fair fluency. In this kind of triggering situation, she had a few options on how to respond.

Call him out on the lie. Acceptable only if she was a friend—and she wasn't, so calling him on it was a sure way to start a fight. She wasn't looking for that either.

Or she could ignore what he'd said and just keep the conversation going in a way that made clear she'd picked up on the lie. Spotted a weakness. Another great way to make friends.

Or, what seemed smartest, pretend to misread the situation and make a joke out of it. Give him an out, assuming he had a sense of humor.

"Did you sleep with Treadwell's daughter or something?" She squinted dramatically at him over her bags.

"No!" He answered so sharply some of the color came back to his cheeks and she felt that moment of vulnerability pass. "He doesn't have a daughter."

"Okay, you did something else, then," she announced. "You just like to speak about as much as *no one* I've ever met."

"Don't care."

She rolled her eyes and shook her head.

"Fine, Miss Congeniality." She jerked her head toward the cabins. "I'm going to continue moving in. Then I'm going to pack my duffel with some weight to simulate the pack carry and run the forest track. And since I know you're not making any other friends with that effervescent charm, you're welcome to take the other room in the cabin if you'd like to sleep somewhere that won't put a crick in your neck. If you don't want to sully a bed, use the couch. Or the floor. I can step over you. No problem. I doubt I'll even *accidentally* kick you more than once or twice. Three times tops."

The pack carry was the second biggest thing she worried about doing sufficiently well. The problem that took up most of her overly developed worry centers was her application mistake—her skydiving experience. Good intentions didn't counter bad planning follow-through. Filling out the application on behalf of her future self—the one who would've completed the training program and gone on several jumps—was only okay until life and family emergencies had interfered with her training schedule. Now it was a lie. In writing. Even if skydiving experience wasn't required to get into the program, once she'd been selected—months later—she hadn't been able to figure out how to rewind it.

She'd gladly run herself ragged with a heavy pack to keep from thinking about those possible consequences.

He levered himself from the ground. "Don't weight your pack for the run tonight. Hard track to run in the dark."

"You think I'll fall?"

"You wanted advice. Don't take unnecessary chances," he said, dusting some of the grass from his…very firm backside and meaty, manly legs.

Then he said more things and screwed up her mental appreciation.

"Washing out already would mean another year before you could get back."

She had wanted to hear advice. *Did* want to. And this was even advice that he didn't stumble his way through or have to force out. It sounded genuine.

It also sounded like *criticism*. *Already* was a very judgmental word. Although she couldn't stop her hackles rising, she was almost thankful for it. Handsome wrapper over a jerky nougat center? He was suddenly far less attractive.

"I'm used to tougher workouts than a woodland path."

"Uneven terrain." Still doubting her ability to

run on shaded trails, and not answering her invitation. Which was fine. Let him sleep in his truck.

He rolled his shoulders and took off at an easy jog for the all-terrain course where he'd sent the others a while ago.

The course was two and a half miles around, two laps to make it five.

If she hurried, she could stash her stuff in the cabin and catch up with him. Then he'd see how sure-footed she was. No falling. Not today. Not tomorrow. Not *already*.

And she still kind of wanted to trip him.

CHAPTER THREE

BECK'S FEET HIT the ground in a steady rhythm, broken only by the need to readjust his step as he covered the uneven packed earth winding through the various pine, fir and tan oaks of the evergreen forest.

Ahead of him lay the only thing he'd looked forward to when considering his return to camp: the gnarled tan oak near the halfway mark on the trail. Tan oaks littered the state, but he loved the ones that were twisted and gnarled. He'd developed an odd affection for this particular ancient-looking tree two years ago and come to think of it in anthropomorphic terms—*the Old Man*.

It was almost all boughs, branching at less than three feet from the ground, a hollowed palm with six fingers shooting toward the sky. A great sitting tree, like the one he'd grown up with in his yard. Shaded. Quiet. A respite from the heat. Surrounded by birdsong. Peaceful. Somewhere to forget where he should've been and wasn't.

Treadwell thought he was being obstinate or stupid, or that it meant he just didn't care about anyone else on the team. Every time he'd gone outside protocol, it had been for valid reasons. Lifesaving. Following the signs he'd seen.

Or thought he'd seen.

Maybe that was the problem. Maybe he hadn't seen anything, just imagined it.

He climbed into the center of the old tree and leaned back on the thickest limb.

If it hadn't been for his fire, he might have just become a forest ranger full-time.

They should've asked for advice about that. He had better words there.

He tilted his head back to gaze through the canopy to the patches of twilight sky. He should've kept the radio on him to keep tabs on the fire and his team.

Before he'd had the chance to fully relax, the sound of someone running far too fast over the packed earth had him tensing. He didn't even need to look to know who it was. She'd run hard to catch up with him, fast enough that she'd have probably caught him even if he hadn't taken a seat.

She skidded to a halt, the sound pulling his gaze from the sky in time to see her toe catch on a root, and she stumbled.

Without thought, he leaped from the tree,

hands shooting out to make a grab for her, but she was just out of reach as she took several large, barely controlled steps forward, and managed to keep from hitting the dirt anyway.

"Okay?" he asked, still covering the distance and giving her a hand to ground her as she recovered her balance.

The touch of her hand sent a surge of lust and heat down his spine that had every muscle tensing.

She froze in place, her eyes wide and locked to his where they stood, facing each other, one hand held between them as if they'd gone to shake hands and had forgotten step two.

Even in the low, fading light, he was once again struck by the color of her eyes. Vibrant, and familiar somehow.

"Fine," she answered, finally looking down to where their hands joined. He followed her gaze, and saw his thumb slowly stroking the back of her hand.

Immediately, he let go, and stepped back, mentally scrambling through a very short list of appropriate things to do or say after doing something so creepy.

She beat him to it. "Not running?"

Still winded, her speech—short as it was— came out broken with her need for oxygen, or maybe with something else. The same words he'd said to her when trying to get rid of her earlier.

She stepped into a shaft of fading light shining through the trees, a brighter spot in a darkened forest, and he could see how flushed she'd grown from the hard, uneven run.

Pretty. Damn, she was appealing in a way he hadn't remembered.

"I'll do two more laps when I get done here."

"Getting late."

"I've run this trail in the dark."

She put her hands on her knees, and her breathing got a little slower, more even, but she still had a wariness about her as she watched him. "This year?"

She had a point, as much as he'd prefer to pretend otherwise. But if he ran with her, this would definitely turn into a competition.

"You know this isn't a race."

"I know."

"But you were running like it was."

"I was running to catch up, not to win."

Bull. He turned and began jogging down the path again, letting her once again catch up, which she quickly did.

"Why are you rolling your eyes at me?"

"I gave you the advice you need to hear— this isn't a race. Neither is it when you're out in the thick of it. Staying longest, fighting hardest, that's important. Not getting there fastest."

"I know that, I've been a firefighter for six years and I was raised by firefighters. Generations of them, actually. I'm not stupid." She kept up with him, but if he'd wanted to pick a way to make her stop with the optimism, he'd apparently picked well, judging by her tone.

"But you're still acting like this is a competition you're in. Work on improving yourself, not impressing everyone else."

He shouldn't have taken a seat tonight. He should've waited until tomorrow, or come back after the run was finished. He'd been wanting to wipe his mind clean, not think about her sun-kissed skin and brilliant green eyes. With his eyes on the trail before him, he suddenly had the strong mental image of a glossy, bright green stone with deep, evergreen bands.

His mother's pendant.

And the same stone as the polished orbs she'd meditated with. Also the polished and raw pieces of gem she'd kept tucked into nooks all over their cottage.

Malachite, the word swam up from somewhere. Healing stone.

"Are you being contrary because you're worried about your crew being out?"

God help him, if this was how the conversation was going to go, he'd be better off trying to lose her. He didn't answer.

"I'm going to take silence for a yes."

"I'm sure they're fine." He was the one in danger of resetting the safety record most recently, not that she needed to know that.

"But it must be hard to be stuck here with the rookies when they're out there."

She was going to ask. He could feel it. And once he gave her a scrap of that information, she'd keep pressing until she got more. Until she forced the conversation he hadn't even wanted to have with Treadwell.

As much to stave it off as to just get the task complete, he picked up speed. A vigorous run was never good for deep conversation.

She kept up.

He glanced to the side and found her facing forward, eyes on the path. At least there was that.

She didn't ask again, but the cadence of sneakers on compact earth began to sound too loud, too heavy.

"We're careful. Haven't lost anyone in a long time." He spoke truth, words that'd probably comfort her, even if she should be afraid of the fire. Everyone should be afraid before they leaped in. "But I should be there."

"Fires come earlier every year. There was always a chance the call could come while you were at camp."

"So?"

"So, you can't do everything."

He snorted.

"What?"

"Funny, coming from someone who wants to be the best at everything."

She didn't say anything to him then, but he could hear her muttering under her breath. When he looked over, he saw her shaking her head and staring ahead like she could happily murder him.

"What?"

"You don't get it. I *have* to be the best." The words came out and she piled on speed, borrowing his tactic.

She didn't get to drop that and run away.

"That's crap," he said when he pulled level again, although the more they argued, the harder the run became. "There aren't tons of women in the service, but there are some and they're treated the same."

She didn't slow down, kept up the speed even when she had to leap roots twisting over the path. "Have you asked them that?"

"Asked them what?"

"If your perception matches their experience."

He stopped running. Did that mean something had happened to *her*?

She slid to a more graceful stop and looked back at him. "We're not supposed to keep taking these breaks."

"We weren't required to run," he reminded her, wanting to ask, but also not.

She thought for a second, then shrugged and propped her hands on her hips, breathing deep and fast, waiting for him to answer the question she'd dropped.

"I don't socialize with them." Or anyone else. This was the most he'd chatted with anyone that he could remember. At least anyone that wasn't an animal.

"I noticed."

"So I never asked them."

"Hence my point. How can you know what they experience without asking when you see them for only short periods and don't talk to them?"

Another point.

"I don't know," he said finally, because the truth sounded a lot more pathetic. He was usually pretty good at reading people, and leaned on that ability to keep from having to ask questions. From having to talk. From having to get *involved*.

She looked at him for a long second, then nodded, and jerked her head in the direction they'd been running. "Offer of couch or cabin still stands."

"Why?"

"Because it's the right thing to do." With that, she got back up to pace, leaving him to run a few yards behind and consider his options.

The idea that anyone would be treated unfairly bothered him, even though he'd seen it frequently enough in life. It jarred with the whole team life Treadwell pitched. It also didn't line up with what he wanted the service to be. A teammate, though temporary teammate, was offering him a place to sleep.

It might not be so bad to take the couch she offered. But it would be dumb, if simply touching her hand made parts of his body go tingly.

Last time he'd brought a tent and never shared quarters with anyone, using only the communal showers and dining facilities when he was awake and not actively sweating to death. Having any roommate was a step up from that, proof he was trying to be a team player. But volunteering to room with the woman who'd made him *see* her as a woman, not just another coworker, would be the kind of stupid Treadwell already seemed to think him.

As they neared the end of the second lap, about to cross their five miles off for the evening, he sped up to catch up with her so she wouldn't leave immediately when she stepped off the path.

"Hey." He touched her arm to stop her, but

as soon as he did, the words he'd wanted to say left his head. Her skin was so hot and slick... firm...

The touch of his hand, no matter how quickly he drew it back, stopped her in her tracks. She turned slowly back to face him, and stepped forward one pace, breaching that bubble of empty space he usually kept around himself. Out in the open air, the last light of day was fading, but the lights on poles around them buzzed, beginning to burn, and he found those astonishingly green eyes staring back at him.

The calm he'd been seeking tickled at the edge of his perception, like a hint of honeysuckle on the night breeze, and he wanted to touch her again.

Swallowing, he took one step back.

"If someone dumps on you because you're a woman, tell me."

As soon as he'd gotten the words out, before he saw more than her little ears pulling back as her face lit with surprise, he stepped around her and jogged off. It was almost chow time, and he was hungry and in need of a shower away from honeyed golden skin and perceptive green eyes.

No way would he take her up on the invitation to share a cabin. He was used to roughing it. Sleeping outside in a sleeping bag hardly qualified. He'd wait for his cabin assignment.

* * *

The next morning, Beck awoke in the cab of his truck, neck stiff and head clogged with thoughts he generally avoided. He'd dreamed about her. He couldn't even remember the last time he'd dreamed about a woman.

It wasn't one of *those* dreams, it wasn't even her pestering him with a million questions. They were just sitting on the porch of his little cottage, playing cards and drinking beer, and she'd kept looking over the top arching edge of her red-backed cards, her eyes even greener for the proximity, and flashing mischief.

There was something very sweet about it, although even trying to explain why just left him wanting to call it boring. Boring dream. Cards. Beer. Porch. Stupid thing to dream about. He'd rather have had some kind of wild sex dream about her. If he'd taken her up on the offer to sleep in the other bed in the cabin she'd claimed, he probably would've had something more cinematic in his head last night.

So he was up early, and made it to the dew-covered field just as the sun came up. Mist still rose from the grass, the morning siren hadn't even blasted, but a few other folks were coming down from the cabins.

"Here."

Her voice came from the side suddenly, and he

turned at the waist to see her, his neck refusing his order to turn. She looked as fresh as a daisy, and had a steaming paper cup in each hand, one of which she held out. "I don't know how you like coffee, but there was a coffee maker in the cabin, and I doubted you had one in the trunk."

"Truck," he corrected. The quirk of her lips said she'd knowingly made that verbal typo. He probably *did* look like he'd been sleeping in a trunk.

"Black, but I have sugar in my pocket," she added.

God help him, he'd bet she did. Sugar. Sweet, addicting sugar...

"I like it black."

"Thought you might. You probably also like it a week old when it's condensed down to an inky liquid you could use to strip an engine block."

"You'll get used to roughing it." He took a sip with some effort, the bitter shot of liquid a fleeting wake-up jolt. "Men in my unit used to pack coffee grounds in their lower lip like tobacco when on guard duty."

"Gross."

"Or chew coffee beans directly."

"Double gross."

"When you're tired enough and the threat of a court-martial rides on you staying awake..."

She smiled at him then, and he really looked

at her. Even in the low morning light, it was the first thing he saw. Malachite. Beautiful. She was girl-next-door cute, but her eyes…

He took another drink of his coffee. Talk. Ask her something. Just stop thinking. She liked to talk. "You're not former military."

The siren blast that called everyone to morning PT startled her, causing her hand to jerk, and heavily creamed coffee sloshed over the side.

"Should've warned you," he said, watching her grumble and shake the liquid off her hand. "Every morning. Get used to it."

"I'll get a sippy cup," she muttered, wiping her hand on her hip.

He grinned at the image, so opposite from the tough exterior she portrayed. Cute. Funny. Able to laugh at herself. That was something new.

When he opened his mouth to comment, the sound of movement behind him had him turning. More folks streamed in, but nowhere near as many as there had been yesterday—the teams were still out. Treadwell, however, was back. He walked in from the main buildings.

"Wasn't sure they were back," he murmured to Autry.

"Looks like he just got here."

The observation wasn't wrong. Treadwell's hair had the spiky, sweaty quality of a head that had spent hours in a helmet being baked from the outside, and the sturdy, vibrant man from yesterday looked like he could've been knocked down with a breath.

"Does he always look like that after a fire?" She kept her voice low, for his ears only.

A closer look and the contrast between the man he saw and what he expected immediately concerned him.

Without another word, he broke away from Autry to catch the chief before he got to the group.

"Everyone okay?"

It was indirect, and the least offensive way to find out if Treadwell was well. Start with the crew, work his way back.

"Had to put Kolinski in charge for this one," Treadwell muttered, shaking his head. "Never seen one so bad so early."

The answer was both oblique and telling. "I can take these guys this morning if you need to catch some sleep."

The old man smiled at him, the first time in a long time, and for the moment he felt like he was doing things right. "I can make the morning PT, son. Might take you up on it for the afternoon. I'm passing you lot to the other trainers for classroom time after. We're hitting the tower."

"So soon?" The tower usually came in the second week.

"I want to make sure everyone's ready for the season as early as possible."

Translation: he thought they might need to pull in some rookies early. The fire must be really bad.

He looked north, and with the brightening sky, even a forty-minute flight south of the wildfire, he could see haze against the pinks and blues of dawn.

Treadwell started forward again to begin PT.

When Beck looked at Autry, he could see the concern still there. He hesitated only a moment, then moved back to her side to continue their quiet conversation. "It's a bad one."

"Did we lose anyone?"

We. She'd already invested, even not knowing anyone. He could hear it in her voice, and although the same worry creaked down his stiff spine, he knew how to divorce himself from it. To keep making good decisions. It was anyone's guess whether or not she could.

"He would've said. He didn't. But we're hitting the tower for classroom today."

"What?"

Her voice, far more shrill than its usual pleasant timbre, drew his gaze.

"You don't want to do the tower?"

"We haven't done the pack run yet." He could see her trying to moderate her reaction, waving a hand as if to dismiss the alarm still there in her features, even though her voice had dropped down off the treetops.

Afraid of jumping? That would really get in the way of the job.

Couldn't be that.

"You're getting worked up because the schedule is different than you expected."

She cleared her throat, waved her hand again and finished off her coffee. "I'm fine with it."

Bull.

"Wouldn't be surprised if the pack run was this morning's PT." He let her off the hook, but then they quieted to listen as Treadwell announced they'd be doing a body carry around the track this morning.

"Or not."

The chief asked if there were preferences for partners, and he glanced over just in time to see her hand shoot up and point to him once and then at herself.

"Ellison and Autry." The chief marked their names on the list.

"You want me to carry you?"

"No. I'm going to carry your grumpy butt," she answered without pause. "Your neck and your night in a trunk would make it hard for you to carry anyone."

"I don't need to be carried."

"Shut up, Beck."

She used his first name, and rather than annoying him he found himself smiling.

"You're pushy, Lauren."

"Damned right I am. I grew up in a fire family who still don't want me to serve. Dad's chief in our house, and my three big brothers are also all in the same station. I'm surprised you don't know that."

"You're the one who's been obsessed with me the past two years."

She paled then and in response shoved him with one hand, just hard enough for him to sway a little. "Shut up. I wasn't obsessed. I just remembered. And then your name was everywhere, like the universe was *gloating* at me."

"I see. I don't know what you mean about my name being everywhere, but whatever you say." He didn't usually tease people. Or play. Or flirt. Crap, he was flirting. What was even being talked about before he started down this alien path?

Her family at the fire station…

"Why would I know about your family?" he asked, but Treadwell blew his whistle, calling everyone to the track.

"Autry's kind of a legendary name in the fire service. Maybe in the forest service, it's not."

He didn't pay attention to that kind of thing,

which he almost regretted now. It sounded like they'd paid no small part in turning her into a tight little ball of competitive energy.

Which he hoped didn't mean she'd over-extended herself by volunteering to carry him.

"I'm heavier than I look, you know."

"You look like you're made of lead." She finished her coffee and held out her hand for the empty cup he was also holding. "See if you can make it to the track, iron man. I'll meet you there."

"You know if you drop me or crap out, we're both in the muck."

She turned around, shoulders popping up. "Trust me."

Easier said than done. But the truth was, she'd be the one getting a strike if she couldn't do it, he was already in. If anything, Treadwell would look upon him allowing her to carry him as a mark of his team spirit, especially as it was the most undignified position. Especially when she was almost a foot shorter than he was, and at least sixty pounds lighter.

Regardless, they were soon both at the track, Treadwell saying, "Once around, Ellison. Don't drop her."

"I'm carrying," Autry corrected, making the chief pause and look her up and down once, then shift the same measuring but obviously tired look to him.

"I told her I was heavy."

"And I told him to trust me," she countered, and then slowly turned to look across the track, three lanes in, where two of the guys were snickering, and he remembered the name of neither of them. It took her turning for him to pick up that they were laughing *at* her. At the idea of *her* carrying *him.*

This was it. This was what she'd been talking about last night.

They weren't snickering out of concern, it was a joke to them. They didn't think she could do it.

He felt a whiff of shame as the next thought crystallized: he'd questioned whether she could do it too, even after she'd said it. Still questioned it, had only made a decision to trust her, which was something he'd never do with the bozos, now doing the far more obnoxious version of what he and Treadwell had just done.

After his offer, he couldn't let it stand, regardless of the state of his neck.

Beck surged forward, ignoring the stiff, pinching pain in his neck, and didn't stop until he was chest to chest with the one who had laughed the loudest. "Problem?"

The man stood up straighter, meeting his gaze

and holding it, a challenge there. Briefly, then he took a step back, not saying anything in response.

It was always a gamble in a crowd of tough guys, going straight for the most aggressive maneuver, but whether it was Beck's seniority or the amount of disgust dripping off him, the man backed down.

"She's really small," he said. "If she can carry you around the track, I'll buy her a case of beer."

"Yeah, she's shorter than you, and she's probably tougher," Beck replied, not backing off yet but not escalating things. "Don't bet against someone on your team, jackass."

"All right, you two." Treadwell sounded weary, but the chief's words were enough to bring them back to their corners, which was when he noticed Lauren looking at him strangely. Like she either couldn't believe what she'd just seen or didn't want to.

"Runners, pick up your wounded. Once around the track," Treadwell called, and then added to Lauren, "Don't drop him, no matter how annoying he gets."

"Yes, Chief."

Was she annoyed? He'd told her he'd have her back if someone started giving her grief.

He didn't have time to ask, or even to suss it out. She grabbed one of his wrists to control the lift, planted her shoulder a little roughly right in his middle to fold him over, and slowly began to lift.

It didn't take more than a second for his density to become apparent. There was a moment where it seemed she wouldn't be able to straighten her knees, but with a grunt and a wobble made it fully up.

His natural reaction was to make sure she really wanted to do this, but even thinking the words made him feel like the jerk who'd been laughing.

There was nothing funny about this. Her butt was perched right there in front of his face because of the way his longer torso hung over her shoulder, and he got a really good view of it, up close and personal.

She'd chosen gray gym shorts that were loose enough to allow free movement—not exactly baggy but not tight either. Short enough for active freedom but not indecent. They were perfectly ordinary cotton shorts, but up close they might as well have been a bikini. He could do nothing but look, because talking had been hard enough when they'd just been running through the woods, but now with her carrying his heavy weight? The best thing he could do for her would be to shut up.

And the best thing he could do for himself was

ignore the way her bum jiggled as she began to walk. To walk too fast.

"Not a race," he reminded her rear end.

"You're heavy, need to hurry."

Her voice showed strain, but she still kept going, and any thoughts for his own dignity faded against the jiggling reminder of her femininity taking up much of his vision.

There was a mole at the top of her left thigh, just below the hem of her shorts. The tingling resumed in his...

Damn it.

He closed his eyes to picture less pleasant things. Moldy bread. The smell of roadkill...

They needed to make it around the track once, the regular track. One quarter mile. But by the first bend she shook with the effort and he'd grown tense all over, trying very hard not to let his body show how pleasant he found hers.

Her stride became shorter and her steps less quick. No matter how fast she wanted to go, physics couldn't be ignored.

Focus on that. Being dropped and her washing out of camp weren't sexy.

"Easy." He should help somehow. There was nothing he could do about his weight, but he could make himself more stable and easier to carry. Decision made, he wrapped his free arm around her hips to stop bouncing around and she wouldn't have to engage her core so deeply to carry him.

"Hard." She grunted the one-word response.

He was significantly heavier than the pack she'd likely trained for. He was also awkward. This was a harder test than the pack, even at the drastically shorter trek.

"Your dad would be proud of you doing it."

It seemed like the supportive thing to say. Call on fond feelings, a desire to make people who loved her proud of her accomplishments. And it did seem to bolster her strength, though the grip she now had on the back of his thigh suggested it wasn't with warm, happy feelings.

Dad wasn't a good subject. Dad who was a chief in her firehouse. And this suggested he wouldn't be proud of her or she didn't want him to be.

This was going to be a spite victory. If they made it around.

She made it to the second bend, and three quarters of the way around the track on determination, but made it the rest of the way with far quicker steps, and with one foot over the line, bent to let him down.

And then kept on bending, to sprawl on her back on the packed earth and fine gravel.

"Good work," Treadwell said, just as Beck reached down to drag her back to her feet.

She clearly didn't want to get up, despite how uncomfortable it had to be, lying on little rocks, and he had to drag her.

Once on her feet, he returned the favor, wedging his good shoulder into her middle until she folded over, and carried her a short distance onto the grass to let her down again.

"Still the first around." He nudged her once again prone body on the still-dewy grass.

Her breath was great, chest-expanding gulps, and she could've probably blown up a Zeppelin in one go. But it was slowing. "Yay, us."

She went to clap, highlighting the trembling, uncontrolled quality to her movements.

"Do you get low blood sugar?" he asked, suddenly concerned she'd exerted herself too much before breakfast.

"No." She held her hand up to him again, and he took it to help her sit back up. "Just over-exertion. I think I was wrong. You're not an iron man. You're that hairy one with the metal bones."

CHAPTER FOUR

HER WORDS MADE Beck laugh, even if it smacked of a slight rebuke to his grooming habits. "I'm the hairy one?"

He was touching her again. He couldn't seem to stop doing that. The carry had been outside his control, but was this the second time he'd touched her hand? Third? He wasn't inexperienced with women, but he'd long since given up on the concept of relationships. His celibacy was a choice, and not one that usually required conscious thought. He normally didn't have to think about the way touching a woman made his perception shift.

Celibacy was easier than this, generally. Not something he kept *thinking* about. Touching her when she was teasing him? Confusing.

"Tell me you shave regularly when you're going into the field. Can't imagine a respirator making a seal over that scruffy face. And the hair on *top* of your head? You've really let that grow wild since you left the Marines."

"My hair doesn't make me heavier." He wrapped his fingers more tightly around her hand and hauled her the rest of the way up, then let go. "Walk. It'll help."

"I think you're full of crappity-crap." She wobbled but still began to walk and he walked with her.

Three steps and her upper arm impacted his, and she stayed there, slightly leaning, taking the steadiness he had to offer.

She was sweating, and he could feel the bone-deep shaking transferring through the shoulder pressed against his upper arm, and all he wanted to do was sling his arm around her waist. Not just to help but to anchor her there against him. Close. Keep on walking until they were alone, and find out if he could distract her as well.

"If I fall, tell Treadwell you tripped me."

Not currently distracted, still joking.

He should follow her lead and get his mind out of the gutter, but her mention of Treadwell did that just as well. His eyes landed on the chief, and the warm, fond feelings he'd been experiencing turned due to the general colorless, almost sagging quality of the man. "He needs to sleep."

"He looks bad…"

There was a grayness to his face that had both of them heading closer, her steps straightening so that she no longer leaned, they no longer touched.

It helped him focus, or maybe the alarm tightening his shoulders did that.

"Chief?"

Treadwell held up one hand to make him wait and Beck held his tongue as the last two teams staggered across the line. Treadwell marked his clipboard and immediately handed it to Beck, as he had done yesterday.

"Partner assignments."

"Partners?" Beck repeated.

"We're buddying up this year." Treadwell topped his answer with a look that added weight. "Everyone is safer in a team, son."

Oh, hell.

Beck wasn't prone to thinking the world revolved around him, in fact he knew the world overlooked him more often than not, but with the specific complaints Treadwell had about Beck's performance within a team? His lone-wolf tendencies and *this* change, *this* year?

He'd heard the *everyone's safer* speech at least ten times now. They were buddying up because Treadwell wanted to teach *him*.

This was about him.

"If someone fails because they're physically incapable, that's one thing. If they fail due to a failure of partnership, then both get a strike. Then it's baseball rules."

"Three strikes?" Lauren asked beside him, sounding a little better.

"Yes." Treadwell then nodded toward the mess hall, where several kitchen workers in white with large trolleys loaded with brown sack breakfasts were plowing in their direction. "After breakfast, announce the partnerships. Partners and cabin-mates. Trainers Ying and Olivera are leading at the tower. Then the pack carry."

In one day? He held his tongue. "Are Ying and Olivera leading the pack carry?"

"You are."

Treadwell walked off toward the cabins before Beck could ask if *he* needed an arm to lean on.

As much as he sucked at teamwork, his failure tended to go in one direction: he could help others, but had never been able to accept help in return. He could help his chief, even wanted to, despite everything.

Treadwell's stride wasn't steady. He wobbled almost as badly as Lauren had.

The ever-powerful leader stooped, as if he didn't have the strength to hold himself to his usual shoulder-squaring attention.

Because of the warning in his head, he didn't look away until Treadwell had slogged up the wooden stairs to the cabins and disappeared.

Lauren's voice came softly from beside him. "Did he say how he was feeling?"

"Just that he needed to sleep."

"Last time I saw someone that color, it was heart-related."

"Me too," Beck muttered. "But I'm going to let him rest, see if that helps, before I start prodding."

Clearly, she wasn't onboard with letting the chief go while looking somewhat corpse-like. "Worried about his pride?"

"Respectful of him as a person." Beck looked at her then, and turned fully, what had nearly gone down earlier before she'd carried him coming back to his mind. "I owe you an apology."

He didn't get to the apology before she'd completely frozen, staring up at him, her breath quickening again.

"Why?"

"I didn't take you at your word when you said you could do it. Neither did Treadwell. But no one questioned anyone else carrying their partner." Beck drew a deep breath, pausing to make sure he selected the correct words since even simply acknowledging the mistake affected her. "To be clear, I questioned because of concern you'd get hurt because you felt the need to prove yourself. Like it or not, you *are* smaller than any of us. But you did it. I don't know that I won't make that mistake again, but I'm aware of it now. I'll try."

She nodded quickly, a small, shaking acknowledgment of his words, eyes glassier than they had been, and he knew how much it meant to her to hear it. Despite the emotional reaction, he was glad for having said it. He might be an active disappointment to the chief, but he could be a good guy sometimes.

She took a moment, and had to clear her throat before she asked in a voice that was a little froggy, "What are we doing?"

He finally looked at the clipboard. "Using the buddy system, apparently. Partnering up, on the field and off."

A list, in Treadwell's bold slashing script, of eight sets of names.

Ellison and Autry

Top of the list. Partnered. Sharing a cabin after all the reasons they shouldn't had become clear to him.

Still, the simple thought summoned myriad images of Lauren and beds, and every part of his body erupted with some kind of excited dread. There was no other way for him to qualify it. Excitement because there was no way around excitement at being alone with a woman he was attracted to, and dread because he didn't know what would spiral out of it. He already felt protective of her, wherever that came from. If it was about her gender, her stature, or who she was.

Dangerous. He didn't even need to wonder how she'd respond to his protective feelings. She'd be pissed. Probably kick him in the junk just to prove she could.

"We're together." He forced himself to stick to the topic, then waved a hand to her to follow him toward the group. "Breakfast now. Tower. Lunch after. Then the pack carry. Going to be a rough day."

"How's the fire?" someone called.

What was the man's name? She'd introduced them yesterday.

Alvarez.

"Bad."

"Are they going back out?"

"I don't think anyone but Treadwell came back today. And he'll probably go back later. I didn't ask," he said, and cast aside his own concerns about whether or not the chief *should* go back out. Respect his wishes, and be there to help if the chief was wrong about his limits. That's what Treadwell had done for *him* on that mountain last season. Right up until Beck had smacked face-first into his limits.

"Focus on what's before you. Tower training with Wang and Olivera. I'll explain the rules on the pack after lunch."

Lots of talking. Lots of talking he didn't want to do, but having seen the chief it was something small he could offer.

"Chow time. Eat hardy. Protein first. Drink a lot."

Lauren stayed at his side, though she looked as unsettled as he felt—strange in light of yesterday's invitation to share a cabin. Did it feel somehow like being fixed up to her too?

"Do you want me to announce the names?" she asked, the look she topped her words with clear enough for anyone to read. *I have your back.* Hearing them wouldn't have made the sentiment any clearer than what he could see there in her eyes. She understood and had his back. Not pushing him to change, not joking about his issues, just backing him up. It was a small matter, but made even clearer what his own words had meant to her.

"There are eight pairs. They can read," he said softly, then handed the clipboard off to the nearest warm body. "Check your assignments. Work out who will be moving tonight, but not before the pack carry. Don't spend the energy. You'll need it later."

All through breakfast, Lauren worked at putting the idea of the tower out of her mind because of Beck. She was still warm all over from his heartfelt apology. He was a man of few words, but when he started using them, he could even distract her from all the imminent tower-shaped doom looming before her.

If she'd known how freaking attractive he could become just by saying the right thing, in the right way, at the right time, she'd have put as much distance between the two of them as possible, no matter the things she might be able to learn from him to get better at her job simply through proximity.

Now, with her protein-dense breakfast burrito in her stomach, heading for the place where her accidental lie might be discovered, she was forced to consider the more imminent source of danger to her. If she failed or fumbled through this, they'd know, and she'd be out of there so fast she'd be glad she hadn't unpacked.

Provided she survived the tower without looking like an incompetent fool, she could look forward to dealing with her hormonal reaction to a handsome, skilled man treating her fairly later. Some way that made distance possible. Maybe by making a long list of things she didn't like about him instead of focusing on the things she did.

The morning's laughing meatheads underscored what she already knew: she had to be twice as good for all the men to take her seriously. And how important it was she not put a toe out of line, let alone her lips.

Hormones would have to bow to the wily ways of logic.

Workplace romances weren't smart, even when you weren't one of three women in a group of seventy-six. Having a boyfriend in her workplace meant yet another voice telling her to be careful, to not go to this job or that, not to overestimate herself. Blah-blah-blah.

At least Beck hadn't said anything like that yet. He'd said the opposite, which elevated her passing appreciation with his attractiveness to something that made her heart quicken enough to rival the tower of concrete and cables now suddenly before her.

Beck walked behind her, and she was momentarily sad to not have him there being beefy and distracting. Several stories tall, it had a sideways launch platform to mimic jumping from a plane, and lines running down at slow-floating angles to the ground, designed to simulate the start and stop of a jump, from launch to landing with little drift in between.

Tilting her head back to stare at the top, her inner gyroscope wobbled off center. With how hard her palms sweated, it was good she wouldn't need her hands to stay in the harness.

"You all right?" Beck's question came from

right behind her and she stopped to look back at him.

However stupid she felt for having missed the window to correct her application before it got this far, she'd kept taking a pass on making the correction because it could've been used against her, and history had taught her that when it came to her job, people in authority weren't much inclined to give her a fair shake. She hated thinking that way, so she'd avoided dealing with it, banking on her own skills bailing her out. Back when her skills had just been something in her mind, not something that she had to actually pull off in the flesh.

"I didn't realize how empty the camp was until just now." She'd said the first thing that came to mind, and a look around confirmed that it was only the sixteen rookies and a couple of trainers. "We'd be doing this with all three groups if the others weren't on a jump, right?"

He nodded. "Classroom stuff is universal, reinforcing the basics and more advanced stuff if it's especially beneficial."

The two trainers called them to attention, and began discussing the equipment worn during a jump. She paid complete attention, even though this was all information she actually felt confident in. Hearing what she already knew helped her relax some. Focusing made her feel like she was doing what she was supposed to be doing.

Too soon, the trainers sorted the group, calling only three names. Ellison. Alvarez. *Autry*.

"You three are with me. Suit up and climb the tower. Everyone else is with Ying."

One look toward the other group and she saw Ying leading them all to the three-foot platforms that she recognized from all the instruction she *had* completed before her classes had been derailed by family.

Her stomach bottomed out. They'd put her into the advanced group. Beck had jumped before. She'd wager Alvarez had also, unless he'd *also* had great plans and had answered on behalf of his future self when filling out the application.

Olivera hustled them to the tower. "We're testing technique to see how rusty you are, and if you need to be bumped back. I'll watch from the ground. If you panic and don't jump, you get bumped back. If you swing too much when you jump, you get bumped back. If you don your gear wrong, you get bumped back. Don't be sloppy."

They stepped into the room at the base of the tower and were directed to get into the jumpsuits and the packs they'd have to strap into. She'd also done this before, or the civilian versions of it, and had trained enough to fumble through.

As she pulled the last strap tight, she caught Beck looking at her again.

"What?"

"You're white as smoke," he whispered.

Crap.

"Breakfast isn't sitting well."

Not why she was white, but still true. Lord, she hated all this lying, she just didn't know how to fix it.

She hurried back out to let Olivera check her equipment. He gave the straps a sharp jerk. "Okay, up the tower, don't jump until I signal."

Verdict: not sloppy. She'd passed *that.*

Two more tests.

She could do this. She might even be able to make the partner and roommate situation work for her by asking Beck for fire-specific jump pointers—talk work, not anything personal.

For all her worries, by the time she made it from pack inspection up miles of stairs to the elevated platform the pit in her stomach was gone and everything seemed much more doable.

She *had* done a lot of simulations.

She *did* have the gumption to jump out of a plane over a blazing inferno.

She knew how to jump and tuck her head and arms, how long to count before grabbing the chute to steer it in.

And she would go first. A female trainer she

hadn't met before sat at the top of the tower, whose very presence bolstered Lauren's confidence further. It took no time to strap her into the harness and when the signal came, she took a deep breath and jumped.

A short fall of a couple of meters, then the harness jerked hard enough to rattle her teeth, but she followed through the steps perfectly. Less than a minute later she landed at the levee and was helped to unhitch so she could run back and do it again.

Today wouldn't be her only instruction before she got to the point of jumping to a fire. The service was known for safety and they'd work their way up, practice at the tower first, then move to a number of low-altitude jumps free from danger, getting skills polished before they worked their way up to jumping near fires. That's how it always went. They'd hold that, even with early burns.

Everything would be okay.

CHAPTER FIVE

EVEN WITH GENERALLY keeping his distance, Beck knew one thing about smokejumpers and soldiers—everyone's rookie training was the worst in history. Bragging about something bad was cool if it proved how tough you were.

Even with their embellishments, he'd never heard of a Day Two that had gone quite so hardcore as this year. His own first experience with *Hell Week* hadn't got this hard this quickly. And even today, *his* today, didn't compare to Lauren's. He'd never been asked to carry anyone so much larger and heavier than he was, and that was the start of a day already asking for one hundred and ten percent of everyone else.

With only three of them jumping from the tower, it was a two-hour cycle of physical punishment. Jumping, being released at the end, and running back across the long field to climb another twenty-some stories to the top to hurl themselves out again.

The jump and glide weren't even relaxing. As

easy as they were by comparison to a real jump, it was still very hard on the body. That initial jerk of the harness hurt, and going through it over and over did its own kind of damage. He'd made seven jumps in two hours, and had felt it in his shoulders and back even before carrying that person-sized pack through the wooded trail and twice around the old dirt track.

Hard day.

Now, standing in line for chow in a mostly empty mess hall, he didn't see her anywhere. Everyone else was there except her.

Had she already been and gone?

Sometime between them joking around after she'd carried him this morning and the tower, she'd gone from chatty and cheerful, if struggling with the aftermath of a hard slog, so far to the other extreme he had to wonder if something else had happened that he'd missed. Another jerk getting mouthy? Something worse than the horror of being assigned his partner?

After Treadwell's little bombshell, they needed to talk about whatever that meant. What she expected, what he needed to work on. He'd spent the past two hours mentally composing ground rules to go over with her, but where the devil was she?

It was possible she'd finished far enough ahead of him to have already eaten and gone, especially considering how much she liked being first at everything. He'd just assumed he'd been behind, doing what he did: conserving energy.

But she'd definitely had less energy at the start of the pack carry to conserve than he'd had. If she'd pushed hard down the wooded track…

No, she wouldn't have made that. The body could only do so much.

His watch confirmed an hour left before dinner ended—time to look for her.

Decision made, he headed back out.

Cabin first, and if she wasn't there, the woods. Then figure out some argument to make on her behalf so she didn't get booted for failing the time requirements.

Just as he reached the door, it opened and a dirty, sweaty, red-faced Autry shuffled in. Her hair, which had been neatly braided at the start of the day, now stuck out all around her face like a disheveled lion's mane.

She met his gaze, then lifted one arm and flopped it in a kind of half circle through the air, the sloppiest, most exhausted rendition of a wave he'd ever seen.

"You look like death."

A statement like that *always* merited an eyeroll. She only managed the verbal equivalent—a dry, hollow, "Thanks."

Before she could get around him, he grabbed

her shoulders and spun her around to shove her right back out of the mess hall.

"I'm hungry," she said, but didn't physically resist. Didn't look like she even had the energy to walk, let alone put up a struggle.

"I'll bring it," he grunted, though his own hunger was suddenly gone. He steered her far enough in the direction of the cabin to make the order clear, but a roll of his stomach made him ask, "Did you finish in ninety?"

"Eighty-nine," she breathed, then stopped long enough to look over her shoulder. "Food?"

"I'll bring two dinners. Go."

"You showered already?"

He'd turned to head back inside, but the pang of defeat in her voice stopped him.

Even conserving energy, he was used to hauling that pack around and it had taken him less time than it had two years ago. "Yeah."

The defeat in her eyes twisted into something else, something more bitter. Something more like what he'd been avoiding feeling about himself since last season. The transparency of her emotions didn't do anything to make him comfortable with her ability to hold it together when things got hairy, but how hard she pushed herself made him want to root for her.

She didn't say anything else, just resumed scuffing her feet across the field to the wooden stairs and the cabins above. Treadwell had moved with about the same amount of energy, but her exhausted, splotchy pink didn't worry him like Treadwell's pallor. Autry's ills could be helped with rest and a little TLC. Not that he'd be doing any of that, but he could bring dinner.

Maybe tomorrow he'd bring lunch to check on the chief too.

Fifteen minutes later, he stepped into the small, spartan cabin to find her asleep at the dinette, sitting in a chair but sprawled from the ribs up over the small, circular tabletop, cheek pressed against the faux wood laminate. Possibly drooling.

Man, he wanted to let her just sleep, but if she was going to be able to do all this again tomorrow, she needed to refuel, give her body some protein to undo the damage they'd done today.

Wake her up, feed her, but all the ground rules he'd been planning to lay out suddenly felt like taking advantage of someone too tired to bear another ounce of pressure.

"Lauren?" He said her name gently, then waited. No response.

He tried again, a little louder.

Still nothing. She was *out*.

When she failed to even flinch after a third volume increase, he gave up and barked, "Autry!"

She jerked up, eyes wild and bleary. It took her staring at him for several seconds for coherent thought to show up. Her gaze fell to the take-out containers in his hands, and she held out both hands.

"You sure you're up to chewing?"

Lauren had to smile at the man's tease, even when her fingers failed to close on the box he handed her, twice. He placed it on the table in front of her.

"Be prepared to Heimlich me." She was tired enough to put her face in the grilled chicken and veggies and just start chewing, it'd free her from the arduous task of lifting plastic cutlery, but she still had enough pride to attempt civilized eating.

She could only manage to fumble the lid off her container and to fist her fork like a toddler before dropping it anyway.

It bounced once on the table and would've hit the floor but for Beck snatching it out of the air and handing it back to her.

Today had been hard, but worth it. She'd done fine.

Everything would be fine. There was no one here to tell her otherwise, so any fear she indulged in was of her own making. And that meant she could control it.

"Eat, shower, bed?"

"Eat. Bed." She could barely contemplate not just lying down on the floor of the kitchenette, where she'd definitely fall asleep.

"Fresh sheets are only delivered once a week. They're not coming to change them in the morning," Beck said, watching her too closely as he ate.

"I know I stink, don't beat around the bush."

He inhaled slowly, then shook his head. "Not stink. You're sweaty, but it's not like the stench that was rolling off me."

"My sweat is less stenchy? Good to know."

He looked like he didn't know quite what to say, then muttered, "You smell…like honey and dirt."

The description made her grin. It could've been a compliment, except for the *dirt* part. "You should make perfumes."

"Don't need to. I make bath bombs."

She paused the train of veggies and meat to her mouth, the words taking too much concentration to parse to allow any reaction but the honest one. Disbelief.

"You do *not* make bath bombs."

"They're more like bath salts. Not formed up into some kind of hygiene hand grenade."

"Too bad. Hygiene hand grenade sounds good right now."

"Bath sounds better. It'll help with the soreness."

Bath that took pain away *did* sound better,

but there was something she knew she needed help with.

"Do you think you could help me stretch out my shoulders?"

He looked confused, but said nothing.

"This muscle." She ran one finger along the top of her shoulder between cuff and neck. "Trapezius. It's not much, just help me lift my arms from behind to stretch that. Only take a minute."

He nodded, still looking confused, but continued eating.

"So, you didn't learn to stretch in the Marines. Did *they* teach you to make bath bombs?"

It took him a while to answer, and when he spoke, the softness in his voice told a story of heartache. "My mom taught me."

She didn't even need to ask to know his mother was no longer with him. She'd grown up with that tone, heard it in her father's voice any time he spoke of her own mother.

"I'm sorry," she said, not knowing quite what else to say to the sad direction she'd pushed the conversation.

He looked up swiftly, brows pinching as he visibly scanned the conversation in his mind. She could see him replaying the words. "How did you know she was gone?"

"My mom died when I was five. My father never remarried, still wears his wedding ring, still carries his grief. There's a way of speaking… It's hard to describe."

"Regret," he murmured. "What you're hearing is regret. What happened to her?"

"She developed breast cancer not long after I was born. I guess that happens sometimes with older mothers. She wasn't really old, but she was older than the usual birth mother age twenty-four years ago. Sick most of the time I knew her. I only have a handful of memories, really. My siblings and I stayed with our grandparents for long stretches when chemo knocked her immune system down and she couldn't afford four germ monsters around her, not and keep fighting."

"I'm sorry, echoed." He watched her with such compassion, she grew more certain his grief was fresher. Was that why he'd ended up back with the rookies?

She'd been looking for reasons he'd been grouped with them, and her speculations had ranged from teaching them, to some oddity of numbers, and through Treadwell's irritation with him to some kind of punishment. Beck participating in the pack carry today fit punishment. That was something only rookies had to do. Those who returned for refreshers had already proved they could carry a body for miles.

Something was wrong, and considering the grief she still saw in his eyes…

"So your dad is just very protective?" His question gave her an excuse not to ask, but she wanted to ask. Maybe she *should* even ask, since he was her partner now.

Instead, she ate and stuck to the subject, at least for now. "Because he couldn't protect her, I guess. And my brothers take their cue from him."

"So why are you all at the same station?"

"It's still my birthright. And as annoying as they are, they can't keep me from doing my job. Besides, I'd rather be there with them and at least have a shot at helping than at a different station and hear about some calamity after the fact."

"But you're here."

She nodded slowly. "Yeah…"

"In the off-season, you'll be with the park service. Not with them."

"I know," she said, but had truthfully done everything she could to not dwell on that—she still wasn't too sure she'd be a great forest ranger. She liked being outside, but she wasn't overly informed about trees and wildlife. "I guess I got tired of swimming upstream. I just haven't reformatted my answer yet. Or thought much about it. Been trying not to think about how I'll feel if something happens and I'm not there."

He went quiet, but she didn't see judgment in his espresso-black eyes. That was sympathy. And shadow.

He hadn't offered more information about his mom, which should tell her enough about how much he wanted to talk about it, but she couldn't *not* ask. Not when there was so much up in the air about this man, her partner. Whatever had gotten him in trouble, she had to know.

"When did you lose your mom?"

It was rude to ask such a question and then keep chowing down, so she waited for his answer, long enough she began to doubt whether she had the energy to continue eating and bathe.

"I was ten."

At least fifteen years ago. A long time to not have developed some distance.

Or maybe she was an anomaly.

Her eldest brother had been older than Beck when their mother had passed, but he'd also developed greater distance than Beck had seemed to.

Her family's loving misogyny, if that was a thing, was definitely a manifestation of their loss. Fear of losing her too. Probably the only reason she'd put up with it so long.

But her mother had died a quiet, slow, terrible death. An expected death, finally.

"How did she die?"

Again, a long silence. Was it not wanting to talk about it or pain that kept his words from coming easily?

"Wildfire." The one-word answer effectively wiped everything else from her mind.

"Oh, God, Beck…"

"I don't want to talk about it," he cut in, as if she had anything else to say that could ever be sufficient.

He had been ten. She'd died in a wildfire. Did Lauren really need to know anything else about why the man had joined the smokejumpers? Why he'd gone into firefighting for the military?

Not when she felt the sudden truth of who he was down deep, where she stuffed all things that could hurt her. It didn't explain what had happened to get him back here after he'd been so lauded, but pressing him felt wrong, as did abandoning the topic entirely.

"How do you make bath bombs?"

If she'd had the fortitude to be silent as long as he could, maybe she could've come up with something more sensitive or compassionate to say. But this was related to his mom, and something he might be able to speak about. It felt like a way in. An acknowledgment, but safe.

Beck lifted his gaze from his meal again, but shifted to the mom-adjacent subject, and began to explain the process and ingredients used.

"I've got a batch made. All that's missing is the pine needles. I can get them out back if you want. They'll help the soreness."

"Thank you. That's…" She swallowed nothing, tried again, bypassing the usual denials she'd make to conceal any vulnerabilities. "I could use a little help right now, I think."

"In the future, you'll hear about *Hell Week* from everyone, and how theirs was the worst," Beck said, closing the container on his dinner. "Trust me, you're going to win those misery competitions."

"I did the same things you did today."

"I've never been asked to carry someone so far who outweighed me by so much. Out in the field, it's always going to be a two-person job, barring catastrophe. We have collapsible stretchers for it."

The subject moved on, and they both eased. And what she heard in his voice now? That was admiration. She felt her smile return, along with the strength to get through the rest of her meal.

Beck not only went after the pine needles, he tied them up in a handkerchief to keep them from poking her in the bath, and ran the hot water to mix it all up.

If this was how it was to have a partner who helped instead of held her back, she was in trouble.

It wasn't as if she'd just dated jerks, but any time she'd got involved with a firefighter—who were the men she most frequently encountered—he had invariably been tied to her station, which had left him subjected to her family's pressure. Troy had just been the one she'd most wanted to believe was on her side, and whose preference of her father had hurt the most.

Troy could also be sweet at times, when they'd been alone and only if work wasn't involved.

That was how this was different. That was how Beck was far more dangerous. He was helping her so she could be ready for tomorrow, not giving her reasons to bail.

And if he was doing all that, she could find the energy to get some clean clothes and get her honey-dirty self into the water.

By the time she dragged herself into her room and out, he was back at the table, sitting, staring off into space. "Water's ready. You want to do your shoulders before or after?"

"Before." She stopped in front of him and folded her arms back to press her fists together in the center of her back. "Just pull my elbows back until I cry *uncle*."

His large, strong hands cupped her elbows and slowly pulled back, stopping when she made an accidental, pained noise, so she had to convince him to go a little further. Then repeated from the front, stretching out the muscles that had tightened this morning and never really relaxed.

"Thanks," she said, breathing a little hard because stretching unruly muscles could hurt, and made for the bathroom.

She didn't make it. He caught her by the back of the shirt, wordlessly wrapping one arm across her shoulders from the front to brace her so he could mash his palm against that same, suffering muscle and rotate. He repeated the motion through several rotations on each side of her spine, tracking halfway down her back as she let her head hang forward and used up every last ounce of strength to stay upright when her body just wanted to fold in on itself.

It wasn't long, minutes she'd have paid money and dignity to continue, and he released her. "Don't fall asleep in the water."

She wobbled, then stepped into the bathroom, intent on bathing as quickly as she could before the truth of his words sank in. There was no way she'd stay awake once she sank into that water. Not alone.

"I hate to ask you for another favor when you've been so kind, but I'm honestly afraid of falling asleep in there."

He'd already sat back down, but turned in his chair toward her. "Okay."

"Keep me company?"

Her words had him on his feet like he was actually *made* of energy.

"Lauren, that's not a good idea. You're very appealing, but bathing together... Bad idea. I didn't mean to give you that idea."

He babbled, speaking faster than she'd heard him say anything, and with so many pauses she suddenly understood she wasn't the only one experiencing the strange pull.

If she'd had any energy left, she'd be embarrassed he thought she was hitting on him, but she didn't. She also wished it didn't sound so appealing. Too tired to blush, she waved a hand. "Not asking you to have a bath with me. Just stay there, talk through the door so I don't drown in my sleep."

He shifted from foot to foot, the way she often did before running.

"And how about I forget anything else you might have said before that?" she added.

A slow nod and he sat back down.

Pride took energy. She had none to spare.

A few minutes later, with the bathroom door just ajar, she settled into the steaming, lavender-scented water and it became obvious how bone deep her soreness was and how nice it would've been to just go to sleep there.

"What do you want to talk about?" he asked outside the door.

Him. She wanted to talk about him. His mom. His life. What had happened to re-rookie him.

That was something she should ask.

"We're partners, and tied together. You're probably worried I'll weigh you down after today."

"I'm not."

That'd be a good reason for him to be so helpful, actually. She *must* be tired, not having realized that before.

"Still, I won't. I'm not going to fail this." *You.* She wanted to say fail *you*, because his help—regardless of motivation—felt like a gift. One she wanted to return.

"If anyone fails because of it, it's going to be me," Beck said after a moment. "Treadwell introduced partnerships this year because I'm bad at teamwork."

Bad at teamwork meant something had happened and it had been his fault.

"What happened?"

"Close call. A risk I shouldn't have taken, I guess."

Also not what he was known for. And not full of details.

"What risk?"

"Chased a dog into a fire, got trapped. Had to be rescued."

"Oh." That didn't sound so bad to her. "Did you save the dog?"

"Had to knock him out, but they were able to drop a safety line from a chopper. It was close, though. Fire… Heat rises, makes it hard to fly in near. Put others in danger."

"But everyone made it?"

"Not the point."

At that moment, she wished she could see his face, figure out what he was saying. What did that negative sound mean? Was it directed at himself? Was he angry at Treadwell for busting him down, or was he angry at people coming to rescue him?

"How are you bad at teamwork?"

"Just am."

"Don't ask permission before doing things? Don't ask for help? Don't…?"

"Don't ask for help."

She could understand that one. "You know, friends don't always need to be asked for help. You helped me tonight, you're helping me now…"

"This isn't dangerous."

She picked up the hankie tied up with pine needles inside and shook her head. The hell this wasn't dangerous. She was in very real danger of making a mistake with this man. This man who was clearly thinking things about her too, even if she was supposed to forget that.

Soaking in the water and talking to him? Maybe also not so good for her emotional balance around him.

New plan: wash fast, say goodnight, go to sleep.

She hurried through the rest, dried enough to get her PJs on, and stepped out of the bath to find him still sitting in the chair.

"You've been great tonight. Thank you." The words failed to live up to what she was feeling, but they were the best she had right now. "You don't like to ask for help, I get it. What about if you just order me to do something?"

"You'd hate that."

"I would, but if it's just code for something else? That's different." She hoped so, at least. "We're partners, and even if we weren't tied together, I'd want to help."

"Why?"

She started dragging herself toward the bedroom. "Because you're a good person."

True, but a little shallow compared to the draw to him she felt.

She still didn't know what had changed in him that had caused his mistake. Bad at teamwork and needing a rescue didn't seem like the kind of thing to be punished for as a one-off. If it wasn't, why had she seen over a year of praise for him?

When he said nothing else, she wobbled on to bed.

More questions would have to wait.

CHAPTER SIX

DAY THREE CAME and went in a blur of exhaustion so intense Lauren could only focus on what was before her.

Although it had lacked another pack carry, after Beck had carried her for morning PT, they'd hit the tower twice and those jump hours—while populated by more rookies who'd moved up—had been rough and bracketed by bootcamp-style calisthenics and lots of running.

The physical exhaustion of Day Three built on Day Two, making it easier to ignore the messy other stuff, even if she saw it there every time she looked at Beck.

His mother. A wildfire. And whatever had pushed him into making mistakes.

The only thing they'd discussed had been the way the fire up north continued to grow, and Treadwell's status after Beck had gone to check on him and been told to "mind his own damned business."

Outside work, it seemed they'd both come to

the same conclusion: yesterday had been too intimate and they needed to step back. And that was okay. They'd worked well together, pushed each other even. After hours, he'd shown her how to use the bath salts and she'd soaked her own aches away without asking for anything else.

When Day Four brought something entirely new, both eagerly volunteered.

Just over two hours into the day, Lauren climbed out of the bus that had carried them north to land between the large, raging fire and a subdivision that could be threatened if the winds turned. They couldn't see flames but smoke clogged the air, turning it hazy orange with the sun filtering through, making breathing an act of endurance before they even began the prep work for a controlled burn.

Treadwell was with them today, but looked worn out. At least with them they could keep an eye on him if he did something more physical besides bark orders and whistle too loudly.

In short order, they were all given shovels—the least glamorous part of the job—and set about digging trenches. Digging down, past the brush and other fuel sources, set limits so they could safely section the wide field and burn the tall dry grasses in controlled patches. They started at the road with the goal of reaching the tree line in the distance.

The hard-packed earth demanded every ounce of strength Lauren could muster after days of hard conditioning, and she was glad for the silence in which everyone else worked.

When they made it to the end of their row, Lauren went for water, and when she looked for Beck afterward she didn't see him. He hadn't gone for a drink. Wasn't resting. Hadn't even gotten started at their next location without her.

Suddenly, not having discussed how their partnership would work seemed like a mistake.

One she should remedy. As soon as she found him.

He wasn't on the bus. Behind the bus. In the truck…

Treadwell saw her looking and gestured far down the field toward the trees and she saw a teeny tiny figure with hands on hips, standing there.

Looking at Treadwell again would've been a mistake, he might've had *strike* written all over it from their bad partnering. She grabbed her shovel, another water, and hurried downfield.

She found him examining the tree line and stabbing the ground here and there with the blade of his shovel.

They were far enough away that the bus and trucks appeared to perhaps have been built for ladybugs.

Somewhere she could speak without being overheard.

"Beck?" She called his name on approach, water in hand for him as a way to smooth over her coming critique.

When he looked up, she joked, "We playing leapfrog, or just avoiding the stench of fourteen sweaty dudes digging?"

"I smell smoke. We need to start down here," he answered, not smiling at all to her joking. Also not taking the water she held out.

"Everyone smells smoke. The air quality is flagged red today for the area."

"It's stronger than it was."

"Okay, did you tell Treadwell or Kolinski?" As if she didn't know the answer to that.

"They saw me."

This was what Treadwell meant by bad at teamwork. "Beck, remember the partnership talk?"

"Your point?"

"Treadwell saw you, he told me where you were. Example of not working well with your team."

He didn't roll his eyes, just looked at her long seconds, then resumed stabbing the ground with his shovel to loosen the dirt.

"Autry, come with me to go sniff some trees," she said in her manliest, commanding tone. "See?

Easy-peasy. Then we're still working as a pair, even if we're ignoring the rest of our team."

"Fine," he muttered, breezing over her silly impersonation to explain. "The fire will come this direction, rocket over that brush, and build too fast and hot to be controlled. Digging here will slow it down some. Controlled burns are great, but we should've started here."

She couldn't argue with the logic, even if she knew they were only there *just in case.* They didn't actually expect the fire to blow toward the subdivision. It could, but it hadn't—there was time to take it methodically, not like if they'd been in the middle of a war.

Things he knew. But the man seemed to only have one setting when it came to the fire. Combat Zone. And maybe that's what it was to him…

"I'll let Treadwell know what we're doing, in case he wants to send other crews down. Drink." She threw the bottle at him, and he dropped his shovel to catch it, but did pause his digging long enough to drink it.

This pattern was repeated twice more over the day—them finishing one task only for Beck to wander off to do something else, leaving her to track him down. By the time the afternoon sun was high and baking them all, she wanted to strangle him, or smack him on the head with her shovel.

The fire never arrived, despite shifting winds blowing smoke their direction. Around three, they lit the first section of field and took turns with shovels and hoses, ready to extinguish any escaping cinders. One section cleared, they moved on to the next. Methodical. Even kind of relaxing, once the shoulder-torturing digging was done. She didn't even have to chase Ellison down once the fire started, it fixated everyone's attention.

Which was how Treadwell collapsed without anyone immediately noticing.

She was the first to see when she handed her shovel off to get another drink, and saw the man stretched out on the ground, matting down tall, brown grasses.

"Chief!"

Her call, no match for the roaring fire, still managed to find Beck's ear. She ran for the downed leader's side, grabbing one arm to check his pulse as she did so, and Beck was right behind her.

"It's beating," Treadwell rasped regarding his heart, but he'd gone a terrible gray, and between the irregular, rapid fluttering beat of his heart and the speed of his breathing, she knew two things: this wasn't because of the heat, and he needed some clean oxygen fast.

Beck made it there just behind her, and dug out his cellphone to call 911.

"Don't make me give you mouth-to-mouth." Beck hadn't so much as smiled at her or anyone else all day, but he attempted levity with the chief.

"First year, maybe you would've. Not now," Treadwell gasped from the ground, his voice holding no fond humor in response, just rebuke. "Autry would still be chasing you down if we hadn't lit the field. You'd never know."

"Quiet. Conserve oxygen." She squeezed Treadwell's hand, then looked up at Beck. "He needs oxygen."

"He never listens anymore." Treadwell kept going, sounding more like a disappointed father than an angry chief. But his speech was so broken, she really wished he'd shut up. "Maybe if he hears it from a dying man."

She chanced a glance at Beck to find any spark of humor gone, and worry in his eyes that bordered on grief.

"You're not dying," Beck said, voice a little hoarse, and hung up on the call. He disappeared directly into the supply truck and came out a moment later with a stretcher and portable oxygen.

She grabbed a bag with tubing and ripped into it to hook the nasal cannula over his ears and direct the oxygen up his nose. "No face mask?"

Beck shook his head. "We weren't packed for work. It's a camp bus."

She held the cannula to Treadwell's nose to make sure it was all going where it should be. "Breathe slow and deep."

"Can't," he panted. "Truck parked on my chest…"

"We're far from the road, the lane's blocked by the bus and trucks," Beck said, kneeling to count Treadwell's pulse. "Too fast."

"Tachycardic," she whispered. "Maybe in some kind of fibrillation. Why don't we have more equipment?"

"I don't know," he muttered. "We're carrying him to the street to meet the crew."

An order. A request. Progress, even if he kind of *had* to ask for it.

She helped Beck transfer the chief to the stretcher along with his oxygen bottle, and inside sixty seconds they had him strapped in and were hurrying over uneven terrain for the main road.

Medical personnel usually made the worst patients, and Treadwell kept up the tradition. He wouldn't stop giving Beck hell the whole time they carried him. Even when he could barely get enough air to speak. Even when he gripped his own chest and stuttered with the pain of it.

Sirens sounded, and behind them the rest of the crew had resumed tending the fire under

Kolinski's command—it couldn't be abandoned, even if the chief was mid–heart attack, which was what seemed to be happening.

The ambulance arrived about the same time they did, and took over, lifting their carried stretcher onto their wheeled one and strapping it in.

Lauren and Beck stood back, but if she thought the team would get into gear, they didn't. One of them seemed young. The other seemed frustrated, but he climbed into the ambulance for supplies.

"What the hell are you doing?" Beck barked out when the younger one fumbled with the chief's suit too tentatively to get it open. Without waiting for an answer, he stepped over and grabbed the zipper, jerking it down, then ripping through the T-shirt beneath to bare his chest. As soon as the seasoned EMT stepped over, Lauren grabbed the pack of electrodes and began applying them. She wasn't a trained paramedic, but she knew how to do that.

"What are you two doing?" Treadwell asked.

Lauren ignored him, reaching for the monitor to pull leads, which Beck took over applying with the experienced EMT. To the younger, who stood there doing nothing, she ordered, "Get him a face mask, he needs a higher oxygen concentration. Are you the driver?"

He nodded.

"Then you," she ordered the elder, "get a line in him and we'll do this. With the four of us, it'll go faster."

"Three," Beck muttered.

Whatever, she was charitable enough to include Skippy the Baby Paramedic in the count if he brought a danged mask.

It wasn't long before they could only stand back and watch the squiggling line track across the monitor. Worry tracked across Beck's face.

"Do you want us to come with you, Chief?" Lauren asked, and when rebuffed got all the details from the EMT about which hospital they'd be going to, then let them work.

Beck, as grim as she'd ever seen him, simply stood to the side, waiting. Watching. She could almost see the chief's gasped and panted tirade getting through to the man she'd spent all day not getting through to.

Treadwell wanted the old Beck back. First-year Beck.

Whatever had happened, it had happened last season. People didn't fall apart because they needed to be rescued once. There was something else, and if they were going to survive as partners, or survive in general, he needed to face it. Whatever *it* was.

* * *

The burning was the quickest part of their day. Not long after carrying the chief to the road, it was done.

The local fire department sent a crew to keep an eye on the smoldering remains, and the exhausted rookies settled in for a long ride back to camp.

Although Lauren had avoided Beck on the ride up, for the ride back she climbed aboard the bus and headed straight to him.

He sat sideways, his back against the metal wall, legs on the seat, eyes closed.

With water in her hands, she hooked a foot behind his legs and shoved them off the padded green cushion to make room.

"What the…?" He started to swear, but when he saw her, the words stopped.

He didn't immediately turn to sit properly, and she could see him considering ways to make her move.

Shove her off. Toss her over the seatback in front of them.

Escalation was standard operating procedure in man conflict world, throwing punches were communication tactics. But he didn't do any of those things. He took his time, but eventually swiveled to face forward. "There *are* other seats."

"I know." She handed him the water she'd brought as a peace offering.

As much as she wanted to check on him in the wake of Treadwell's tirade, she'd also reached the point where she couldn't just wait for him to deal with *whatever* anymore. Like it or not, his problems were her problems.

She didn't immediately launch in, just enjoyed some water and waited until they were on the freeway, where open windows and six big tires rushing over asphalt created a sound barrier to keep their conversation private.

"Treadwell's been your chief since you started?" she asked, turning just slightly on the seat so she could watch him.

His nod confirmed it, as did the tilt of his head away from the window. His gaze bored into the top seam of the evergreen seatback in front of them. He wasn't talking, but he was listening.

And he wasn't okay. Upset, and not just because he was worried for the chief—still clearly thinking about the chief's words, a man who truly cared about him but didn't understand what was going on with him either.

Check on him first. Be kind. Make him talk.

"Have you noticed anything up with him before this week? Slowing down? Getting winded easily?"

"Haven't seen him much the past several

months. Like I said, in the off-season I wear a different uniform. Clear trails. Remove brush from the forest. Perform small burns."

The forest ranger part of the job. "You like it?"

He nodded again, but his eyes took on a kind of unfocused quality that told her he was thinking about something specifically.

"What?"

"Maybe Treadwell did have something going on that day he called me in to give me the talk."

The talk. This wasn't birds-and-bees territory, even if Treadwell was starting to feel strangely like Beck's surrogate father. He meant the probation talk.

"Because you're not good at teamwork."

"Don't try gentle criticism, Autry," he grunted, using her last name again, but telling her his frustration was pointed inward. "I know I screwed up."

"Okay." She capped the remaining half of her water, focusing all her attention on the conversation. "So why do you do it?"

"I don't know."

"I don't believe you. You're too solitary a creature not to be introspective. Everyone has a reason for the decisions they make, even if the reason is stupid. Even if the reason is like… executive function issues."

"Executive function…?"

"My middle brother has ADHD, and they call it executive function disorder or something. He has trouble with impulsivity, which basically stems from not understanding why he does the things he does, or that he's being driven to make decisions by his emotions. Like why he shouldn't trade in a car he's had for three months and buy another..."

"He's a firefighter?"

"He's really good at things when he's super-interested in them, and he is at his job. He hears everything, notices everything. If you're with him in a burn, he'll know something bad is about to happen before you do. It's almost creepy, really. It's the rest of his life that he has trouble with." She paused, realizing she was going off at a tangent, defending someone Beck didn't even know. "Point is, I think you know why you do what you do. You have reasons. And if you don't know, you don't want to know."

Beck had a tendency to take his time with any words he parceled out, and he took his time again now.

He didn't have the profile of a man searching his soul. He looked like a man who hated what he already knew about himself.

She interrupted, trying to prompt speech. "How do you see fire, Beck?"

"That's a stupid question. I see it as fire."

"You see it as something more than just fire."

He rolled his eyes. "Fine, what do you see fire as?"

She hadn't really thought about how to describe the difference she saw in her own feelings about fire and his.

It took a moment to summon the imagery, and although it felt stupid to correlate fire with water, she said it anyway.

"I see it like the deep end of a swimming pool, and I'm a lifeguard who's relegated to the shallows. I can see people drowning, but every time I try to help, someone important side-eyes me, hands me water wings and tells me to mind the kiddie pool."

And as soon as she put it into words, the mental images kept coming.

"Or a dance I've been invited to, but only so I can serve the refreshments."

"I get it." He cut her off and turned back to the window in silence.

Was he thinking or shutting her out? Probably the latter, but if she was going to get any kind of answer, she had to give him at least a little time to think.

Outside the windows, other cars passed in a blur of color and faces against a backdrop of gray concrete. It wasn't anything to look at, but she let him look for a long time.

"My adversary," he said finally. "I see the fire like a cop chasing the serial killer that killed his family."

He spoke quietly, and what came out was much bigger than she knew how to deal with. Adversary wasn't even accurate. Too civilized-sounding by comparison. Even hearing him say those words made her chest burn like she'd been inhaling cinders for days.

It was a lot. But it wasn't everything, it couldn't be. His mother had died terribly when he was ten, and two years ago he'd been the star quarterback. Something had specifically changed last year.

She leaned in closer so she could speak softly, as that kind of question should be asked with reverence. "Did your brush with the fire bring all that back? With your mom?"

He looked pained, and then shook his head, repeating, "I don't know."

He didn't know because he wasn't ready to go there.

She couldn't force him to do it either.

"How can I help you on the job? I know the job is important to you. How can I help you?"

"I don't know." He said the words again.

"Does Treadwell know about her?"

He didn't repeat himself, just shrugged, making clear they hadn't spoken of it. There were services that would've been offered to help him if he'd ever asked for help.

"You have to figure this out, Beck. Don't expect me to let up either. I know it sucks to talk about it, to relive it or to have someone trying to make you look at what you lived from some other point of view, but there's something to this and you have to figure it out."

"What other point of view is there?" he bit out. Aggression. An emotional dodge from the manspeak playbook to redirect the conversation. He needed to focus.

"Like how terrible it would've been for your mom had you been the one to die and she to live."

She shouldn't have said that, she knew it the instant the words flew out of her mouth and the meager color he'd regained since Treadwell's collapse drained away.

He looked back out the window, once again returning to his usual broody silence. She wanted to touch him, and probably would have—even there on the packed bus, where anyone could've seen.

In fact, she actually did rise up a little to look around, and saw fourteen other sweaty men sleeping in their seats, and that one jerk who'd laughed at her smirking at them.

Copeland.

He had one brow up, arching in challenge, eyes

full of judgment, and mouthed, "Are you going to make out now?"

Beck turned just then, and caught her staring back at the man, and picked up the sudden shift in tension even though he'd missed the silent gibe. Still, he placed his hands on the seat to rise and confront the man for her.

Having Beck defend her again would only embolden Copeland to continue, get worse. Escalation was the male confrontational hallmark. Besides, she couldn't have Beck taking on another emotional landmine while he was tiptoeing around his own.

Not going to happen.

She sprang up, reared back, and with the half-empty water bottle as her only weapon hurled it at Copeland's head with as much speed and force as she could put into a wobbling, off-center, water-filled plastic missile.

It tumbled end over end, and the heavier, water-filled base of the soft plastic bottle smashed into his cheek. Because she had three brothers, Lauren hit whatever she aimed at.

Instantly, his face went red and he surged to his feet.

She'd learned that look from her brothers too. Confrontation face. She couldn't back down now.

Taking one deep breath, she hopped onto the padded seat she'd just vacated and launched herself at the man, but Beck was faster. He slung one arm across her hips as she jumped and pulled her back into the seat as other, more sensible men near Copeland got in his way too.

"Are you seriously going to fight that ass?" Beck shouted at her, dropping her in the seat. "He's twice as big as you are."

"I don't need anyone fighting my battles, Ellison. And I'm through taking crap from him." She slid to the side, got back on her feet, but didn't launch back in again, just stood her ground.

"No one's fighting." Kolinski seemed to have awakened in the shouting and kerfuffle, and pushed back through to the middle of them. "Did I just see Ellison keep his partner from doing something stupid?"

"Not stupid," she argued, ignoring the small amount of praise slipped in there for Beck, who'd apparently finally exhibited some team spirit by stopping her from stomping on Copeland's dangly bits. "I'm not putting up with sexist crap from that jerk. He's always running his mouth. If you want to nail me for not working and playing nicely with my teammate, look to him as well."

Kolinski turned to look back at Copeland. "What sexist crap?"

Copeland mustered the decency to look chagrined, and went for the traditional sexist cop-out. "I was just kidding. Not my fault she can't take a joke."

When Kolinski looked back at her, she snorted but gave up on the nonsense. It was over. He had been caught out. He probably wouldn't make the same mistake again, and if she hadn't let Beck get in his grill about it last time, he wouldn't have done it this time. "The idea of making out with your partner is hilarious. I'm sure you'd have said it to any of the dudes here chatting with *their* partners."

Point made, Copeland sat and glared out the window, and everyone returned to their seats.

Beck's steely glare leveled at her brought the frustration out that she'd been trying to contain. "I'm just going to add this and then I'll let it go for now. Whether or not we were tied together, it would be wrong of me to let you plod forward like everything was fine without at least pointing out that you're letting your emotions get the better of you in fires. I'm not saying you're imagining danger, or that your actions are increasing the danger to yourself and your team, but, like it or not, if you get stuck, someone is going to come for you. The safety record the service holds is as much about making smart decisions as having the best people."

"This from the woman whose emotions just made her have a Chihuahua-bulldog confrontation?" His voice rose enough that she saw heads turning out of the corner of her eye, and knew that the conversation was done.

"There you go again, thinking I can't handle what I say I can handle. Sort it out, Beck. I like you, I really do, but if you think I'm going to let up, you haven't experienced how tenacious a Chihuahua can be."

She stepped around the next seat forward and sat again. Not with Beck. She wasn't mad at him, she was just tired, and the knowledge they hadn't come to any kind of understanding was the cherry on top of a long, emotion-laden day. All she wanted to do was shower, eat, sleep and survive tomorrow.

One more day of *Hell Week*.

CHAPTER SEVEN

AFTER THE FIELD, after Treadwell's ranting collapse, Beck spent the kind of night where he wasn't sure whether he'd slept or not. Even after hiking directly into the woods upon arriving back at camp, and staying immersed in night song and the cool dampness of the forest. Even in the wooded embrace of his favorite tan oak.

If he'd stayed back there in the woods, he might've been able to sleep. But he hadn't. He'd thought about Lauren's words, and those malachite green eyes that pressed into him, and he'd returned to the cabin to thrash around in his bed until morning. Even if they weren't technically speaking, being under the same roof felt necessary. Probably some residual notion of partnership he'd only just grasped because it was ingrained in the genetic makeup of humans. It certainly wasn't something he'd done out of inspiration.

He'd dragged through the day, exhausted in a way that snowballed, mentally and physically.

There had been news about Treadwell, a mixed bag: he'd definitely had a heart attack and they'd performed an emergency procedure to open those vessels up, but no word had come on lasting damage to the heart. For all Beck knew, this was the end of Treadwell's career. Which would mean a new chief, and one who wouldn't have this positive memory of the things Beck was capable of if he could get his head straight.

And that's what was keeping him from sleep. That and the lingering frustration he had with Lauren after a day of purposeful avoidance, because opening his mouth would prove she'd hit on a sore subject with him, and not talking now probably proved her point. He was too emotional and let it impair his judgment.

He rolled over again and the clock's glaring, judgmental red numbers launched him from the bed.

Just tell her. Tell her what had happened last year, and let *her* chew on it, not him. Get the words out of his own head so he could sleep.

In the dark, he stormed out of his own room and knocked once, hard, on her door before opening it.

She bolted upright, but in the dark he couldn't see her expression. That was good. Then he wouldn't have to read it, or hide from it.

"I'm tired and I just want to go to sleep, but I

can't stop thinking. I don't want to think about it. I just want it to go away. I just want to be busy and not think about it and have it go away…"

"Okay," she said groggily, then fumbled with the bedside lamp.

He launched forward, grabbing her hand before she could close around the key to turn it on, and pushing it back to her lap.

"Beck?"

"I just want to say it and go to sleep. Okay?"

"Okay," she said again. In the dark, he could hear her confused, sleepy breathing, but she didn't sound scared. She would. This wasn't going to make things better.

"There was a local fireman last summer in Oregon when we were called in. He got separated from the group and no one would let me go in for him," Beck said, stepping back from the bed, wanting distance from that too. "They wouldn't let me go, and he died. And I can't… I can't leave anyone behind. I can't do it. It's not in me to do that. If there's a chance, and there's always a chance."

"What do you mean, they wouldn't let you go? You listened to orders?"

"No. I mean…three of them wrestled me into the back of a parked police cruiser and locked me in." He really hadn't had a choice then. There was no opening those doors from the inside.

"Oh." She lifted her hand, almost turned on the

light, but then remembered and rubbed her face instead. "There's not always a chance."

"There is."

"Okay." She tried again. "There's always a chance for a while, but there comes a time when the chance is so small that it becomes a bad call."

"If someone's willing to risk it…"

"That's not your call."

"The smokejumpers who saved me? They bucked orders. They bucked orders and came in anyway."

"Treadwell didn't send them?"

Right. He hadn't told her that.

"Not then. When I was a kid. When the fire came, they bucked orders. There was a chopper, they came after us. That's why I survived. I survived *after* someone decided it was too dangerous to risk." He tried to explain, but it was hard to put feelings into words. "Last year, there was a place where the fire seemed thinner. And there was a clear pocket in the middle where the man was. I could've gone through the fire. Or maybe gone up in a chopper and dropped to him."

"The people who saved you risked themselves to save a *family*. They risked for a family. For a child…" she said softly, picking up the thread of conversation as slowly as she climbed from the bed, the creaking of the mattress and the rustle of sheets distracting. The sound of rustling cotton had never sounded so nice, so enticing.

That's what he wanted, to be distracted. "But you can't think it's smart to exchange one life for another, if there was even a chance that your death could've saved him."

"There's always a chance," he repeated. Without thinking, he stepped closer, hands restless, body restless, mind restless. "They came for a family, and left with a child. They had to leave her. I had to leave her. Do you...? You can't expect that to be something someone can do again. And I couldn't get to him. And now I don't ask permission. I just do what I need to do."

He hadn't actually touched her yet, though he'd reached out and retreated several times during his blathering, but when she took the next step and reached for his shoulders, he backtracked across the room.

"Why couldn't they get to your mother?" She focused in on that.

"Fire moved too fast. It was too late. They couldn't find her, they said." The burnt, scarred trees flashed into his mind, the remains of their cottage, and a lingering bitterness with himself that he still didn't want to believe them. "I guess it makes sense, the fire got all the way to the river."

"You saw it?"

"A couple of years later." Long past the time when anything could've still been smoldering, but that was how he remembered it: with smoke rising from everything. Their little cottage by the river. The trees surrounding it, the forest beyond. Even the grass smoldered in his memory.

Anyone would've picked the river over the flames, but the prospect of her dying in the water didn't make it better.

He'd lied to himself for years about that day, because the images he played in his mind of his mother were of her having *survived* the water. Maybe with a head injury, something that made her forget. No body meant no true ending to her. That was the only thought that actually soothed.

The smokejumpers who'd rescued him couldn't have known their story, true or not, wouldn't be the kinder alternative. Which was its own kind of twisted and sick to think he'd be in a better place mentally, feel less guilty, if she'd died in the flames.

His mother had worn the malachite pendant and crystals had littered their home because she needed their help for something. Something had happened and she'd drawn away from the world, using money left to her by her father to buy land and build the cabin *away*, where it was safe. He didn't know what had made her retreat, had only ever gotten vague cautions from her about the world being dangerous, and had known her to meditate with the malachite when her emotions got out of control. When he couldn't talk her through another panic attack.

Which was why the idea of her drowning wasn't better. He *couldn't* have helped her survive the fire, but if he'd gone into the water with her... There was a chance. If he hadn't let them take him. If he hadn't left her behind. It was torturous to think of her burning alive with him helpless to stop it, but thinking of her drowning because he abandoned her put her death on his hands.

He'd told himself a lie of hope, and during the first years, it helped him get through. Maybe never having found her was kinder than knowing it was one or the other, it left room for the denial that had let him survive. A little boy's dream he could no longer believe, the reason he could never leave anyone behind again.

Lauren stopped following when he reached the doorway, and the next step would mean leaving. In that moment, he wanted to see her eyes. With one hand, he found the switch for the overhead and flipped it on so they were both squinting and blinking against the sudden brightness. When she opened her eyes fully again, there it was. The malachite green, pale in the center, and impossibly dark at the edge of the iris.

Malachite was for healing, he'd looked it up. Healing and bringing hidden pain to the surface.

Probably why he was subconsciously drawn to her. Maybe even why he felt compelled to tell her things he didn't even like to admit to himself. Because not doing so felt somehow like lying to *family*.

"Are you angry with Treadwell for not letting you go in after the firefighter?"

"I don't know," he said, shaking his head again, and this time he really didn't have that answer, and he didn't want to think about that right now, open up new avenues to keep him from sleep. He'd said what he'd needed to say, the things that had been running around in his head, and now he just wanted to sleep.

"You need to talk to someone about this, Beck. Everything about it. I'm more than willing to listen if you want to tell me everything, talk through it..."

"That's it. I don't have anything else."

"That's not it," she said, and there was no slow, gentle approach this time, she just was suddenly right there, her hands holding his face, making him look at her. "If it's not me, then it needs to be someone. Yesterday, on the bus, you said the fire was your adversary. I see it as a thing that's being held out of my grasp, you see it as something living and sentient—a monster hiding behind corners, waiting to take people from you. And I get it. I don't think there's any reason you wouldn't feel that way, with what you've experienced. But you can't outsmart fire. It's not a chess match with a serial killer."

"I know that."

"Do you?" Her hands gave one sharp, small shake, just enough to jostle him and command his focus. "Treadwell was right not to send you in. It was down to deciding if he lost one firefighter or two. And even if the man survived and you died getting him out, that's still bad math. His life wasn't more valuable than yours. The dog you went after later on wasn't more valuable than you are, even if it would've been tragic for him to burn up in that fire."

She still held his cheeks, her touch a spark of temptation that made him want to stay. Climb into the bed with her, take the peace that flowed from her touch.

"I know they called you the Smoke Charmer, but you were wrong about that fire with the dog. You were wrong yesterday when you thought the fire was coming and we should reformulate the digging plan. It didn't show up while we worked. If all that's happened has thrown soot on your crystal ball, then you have to rely on the judgment of others until you get it cleared off. And you need to talk to someone about it."

He stepped fully back out of her bedroom then, and to her credit she didn't chase him, just let go and stood there in the doorway, looking at him with those big, worried eyes.

"Treadwell wants to understand."

"He's ill. I'm not dumping all this on him."

"He'll be back. And if he's not, he still deserves to know what he's been beating his head against. Not understanding what's shifted in you, someone he clearly values, is unfair to him. It's unfair to you."

Unfair to him? He shook his head, refusing to give that another thought. He'd had two days giving everything he had physically, and no sleep. He needed to sleep. If he couldn't sleep now, then he'd just gone through all that for nothing.

A siren blast rocketed through the camp about the same time as the troops were normally called to morning PT, and jerked Lauren awake from sleep.

Heart pounding, one thought came: *I'm late*.

Stumbling from the bed, she fumbled to the bureau, not even needing to turn the lights on to see what she was doing. It was early, but the sun had warmed the skies enough to send something brighter than twilight through her window. She could see shapes, grab knobs to the correct drawers.

Inside, she grabbed blindly and came out with shorts, socks, underthings and a T-shirt, of some random color combination. Her breathing took the form of the kind of labored panting usually accompanying a hard run just from wrestling her uncooperative body into her clothes.

With no time to fix her hair, or anything else, she grabbed a hair band and her shoes, and made it into the main room about the same time as Beck.

He looked similarly wild and out of sorts.

"You overslept too?" She choked the words out while hopping toward the door, trying to cram her feet into her sneakers.

The question stopped him staggering around and he shook his head. "It's Saturday…"

"Saturday?" She fell off-balance, smashing one shoulder into the wall and landing on her bum on the floor as his meaning dawned on her. "We're not late?"

"No."

"They're just messing with us?"

He thought a second, then shook his head. "Doubt it."

"But we're supposed to go to the field…"

He grabbed his own shoes, looking more and more certain. "That's what that siren always means."

They were either being tested and put off-balance for a reason, or something was wrong.

She took the time while on the floor to get her other shoe on, and gathered her hair back as neatly as she could in a few seconds, wrapped it in the hair band and was ready to accept the hand up Beck offered as he got to the door.

"Something happened, didn't it?"

"I think so."

His black eyes had the puffy, sleepy-five-year-old softness of someone who'd slept very hard. At least his midnight confessional had done the trick.

She probably looked no better, and that would continue if this day was going to go the way it seemed about to go.

They ran for the field. Others she recognized from earlier in the week before their teams had been deployed to the hellfire up north arrived at the same time, along with the rookies.

Kolinski jogged onto the field shortly after they got there, and delivered orders. They needed more bodies, but only three rookies had been cleared to go: Beck, Alvarez and *Autry*.

It was still a good couple of miles behind the current side-wall, but wind was a crazy thing and with a storm coming in it was definitely going to change directions. The plan was the same as they'd done Thursday—controlled burns to consume the fuel, but somewhat closer, with a jump to reach it.

Her palms started to sweat, and she did her best to ignore them.

Not a jump *into* the fire, a jump to the *other* side of the fire.

The fire up north had ravaged the mountains all week and had already chewed through three subdivisions and countless thousands of acres of woodland. Where they'd be going was hard to reach, but might keep it from spreading back in the direction of civilization, and that was as good a reason as any to ignore that voice in her head questioning whether she could do this.

Not jumping *into* the fire. The whole mission was skydiving with the goal of digging a lot when she got where she was supposed to go.

That wasn't so bad.

She could do that, even if she hadn't technically ever done the first bit fully before.

She'd practiced with the tower all week. With the months of on and off and simulator training when she'd been unable to actually go up in the air.

Don't panic.

"You all right?" Beck's voice cut through her mental tap dancing to shore up her confidence.

She managed to look at him like he was nuts for asking, because outward confidence was something she'd learned to fake a long time ago with occasional blips. It was the inner monologue she really struggled with, and tried to never let anyone see, past glimpses that made her new partner suspicious.

"Of course I am. This is like…a *jump*! For real. I'm totally ready." Lie. Lie until it's true. "Excited!"

The look he gave her said he bought it about as much as she did.

When she got into the plane, everything would be fine. It was just the shock of wrapping her head around the new, surprising turn of events. And the realization that she couldn't unwind this without doing actual damage to her career. Plenty of motivation to muscle through.

Once she'd made this jump, she'd have that experience she still regretted not correcting on her application. This one jump would set things right, she could actually claim skydiving experience. So it was good. Better than good. She wouldn't have to keep looking over her shoulder, wondering when they were going to find out she had no experience.

Even better, if she went up today, she'd get to help stop the fire from plowing into the next inhabited zone. Protect the families there. Maybe stop from happening to some other kid what had happened to Beck.

The pressure she'd felt in her head suddenly lifted, and her mental pep talk stopped being something she had to convince herself of. She *felt* it and it comforted her. Mostly.

She could do this.

All she had to do was throw herself out of a plane into a great big fire.

No, *near* a big fire. Not in. Near the fire. Everything would be fine.

Then she'd know for sure everyone, including herself, had been wrong about her.

No matter what she'd learned in school, Lauren was now convinced time didn't flow at anything in the vicinity of a constant speed. She'd blinked and perhaps acquired the ability to teleport or bend time. She was suddenly on the plane, fully suited with people moving ahead of her at a steady pace to exit the small, low-flying cargo plane. Their static lines were clipped along the tethers that would see their chutes open when they exited. In the front were the most seasoned, with the rookies—Alvarez, her and Beck—at the end.

He was the caboose on this crazy train, moving behind her so she had to keep going. All she knew was a dwindling line of people that stood between her stupid, trembling body and the open air. And that she couldn't feel her face.

This wasn't a situation where people paused and then jumped when they were ready. It was programmed through all training that you leaped as soon as you got to the exit. So the pace? Her heart was the only thing moving faster.

Alvarez went, which meant it was her turn. She was there at the door, and in her mind she had one leg lifted and ready to spring into the nothing, but instead of tucking, her arms shot out instinctively and grabbed the sides of the port to stop herself.

From high above, even though they wouldn't be landing near the thick of it, she could see the bright glowing reds and orange of the fire and the extent of it.

Throwing herself into a big fire.

Something nudged her from behind, not hard, just a suggestion she go, but she pedaled backward instead, plowing Beck back with her until she was a good four feet from the door.

He shouted something, but she didn't hear it. All she knew was him suddenly moving around her, and hooking his line back in.

When he looked at her again, what she saw made her heart fall further than she would have if she'd stepped out. That wasn't pity she saw in his dark eyes. It was judgment.

He didn't say anything, just shook his head and stepped right on out of the plane, which had her hurtling to the portal again and craning to see his chute open.

There was a certain amount of time in which to jump and stay with your crew. And now she had to go, didn't she? He'd gone. She was his partner. She was his partner and she was leaving him to go down there without someone specifically watching his back. That was definitely a strike.

Crap!

There was no backing out now. She'd signed up. She'd given her word. She'd said she could do the job. If she couldn't jump now, what good was she? She'd fail, not because someone else thought she wasn't up to the task but because *she wasn't up to the task*.

Her stomach lurched and the breakfast they'd all inhaled on the bus en route to the hangar rose up.

If she didn't jump, they were all right about her.

The plane tilted a little, starting to turn back. If she didn't jump now, it was all over.

Before she could let herself think further, before she could miss that window, she stepped out of the door.

Immediately her training kicked in. She tucked her traitorous arms and ducked her head so that brief free fall didn't result in injury or a chute malfunction when it snapped her back and unfurled to carry her aloft over the hellish landscape.

Breathing was harder than she'd expected, some combination of the wind rushing against her face and how hard her heart beat probably. She gripped the straps of the chute and held up, but kept her face turned into her upper arm for a wind buffer until she caught her breath.

Time still meant nothing. She could've drifted down for an hour or a few seconds, however long it took her to get the hang of breathing, then she let herself look around and appreciate the landscape. The fiery landscape.

And the distinct lack of any other parachutes in the sky with her.

Twisting as best she could in the harness, she tried to spot them behind her, but saw nothing. Recalling training advice, she tried to steer herself gently around to spot them, but they hadn't jumped from high up, and when she got the thing spun the direction she thought she'd wanted, the only thing she saw was fire. Rapidly approaching fire.

How long had she failed to jump? It hadn't seemed that long…

CHAPTER EIGHT

DISAPPOINTMENT HUNG AROUND him longer than Beck hung in the treetop he'd gotten tangled in landing. He'd really expected her to jump. She'd projected such an air of fearlessness.

She'd still frozen. He should've seen it coming, the way she'd paled and babbled over the prospect of it earlier. Got too far in her own head. Psyched herself out.

He pulled a knife from his belt and hacked through the ropes holding him up.

The tree he'd hit was two trees past the clearing he'd aimed for, and a quick survey confirmed that the best way down was up one stretch of a branch and around to the back where he could find a better path down.

He probably shouldn't have jumped without her. Did that count as a partnership failure? Who even knew?

He went up and around, using the height to spot where to go to get his suit and supplies. That was when he saw another white chute drifting down, far off target from the zone.

He'd been the last to jump.

His heart stopped cold for a second, and then began to hammer and bang around in his suddenly cold, hollow chest.

It was her. It had to be her.

He'd barely made the jump window, and they'd been flying *toward* the fire, that direction had provided the best with the current wind patterns. And she'd jumped late. She'd jumped far too late.

Damn it.

He was supposed to be climbing down, getting his gear, getting to work, and instead he gripped the branches, holding on, his eyes fixed on her descent to the fire.

She was trying to spin it out, he could see the angle of the chute change as she did her best to steer it, including her legs stretching and twisting helplessly. The wind had her.

She was going down in the fire.

"Ellison!"

A voice barked through his comm. He should answer, but it was one more thing to do when he was barely managing the two things most important for his survival: holding onto the branches and following her progress against the burning mountainside they'd jumped to.

Just when he thought he was going to watch her spiral into the fire, she turned her chute toward the blaze, and straightened out, catching a wind gust. It blew her harder and faster, and maybe farther? Maybe into a pocket?

God, he couldn't tell. All he knew was trees and fire as he saw the white canopy of her chute disappear over the burning edge of the hillside.

"Ellison! *Answer.*"

Hands shaking, he continued to grip one branch but managed to press his earpiece and call out his position. "In a tree. Coming down. Does anyone see where Autry landed?"

He couldn't see anything else from up there. The only thing to do was get down, get suited, and see if there was a path for him to reach her and get her out of the fire. He could pack a suit for her on his back—she was only in her jump suit, no protection against the flames.

He wasn't a praying man, but in that moment he longed for the comfort of such faith.

Why had he jumped without her? He shouldn't have jumped. They were supposed to be partners, and he'd just told her less than thirty-six hours ago that he wouldn't go off on his own.

"She jumped late," someone said over the comm. And then, "Spotter said she's down in a small clearing. Landed hard. Not moving. Not answering attempts to raise her on the comm."

No. No. No. *No.*

"Is she in the blaze?" he asked through the comm.

"Not yet. Unless she doesn't get up and start moving. She has an exit if she's conscious."

He swung down from the tree and scrambled up the downslope he'd landed on to the clearing that had been targeted for landing. His team was there, gathered around the crates dropped with gear and supplies.

If she was conscious, she could either hike out to the nearest road or to another team—maybe one working the edges of the blaze, not at the safer distance of him and the crew.

"Can I reach her?" he asked, hurrying toward the group as they gathered around the dropped supplies.

There was a pause. He reached the group, and Kolinski, owner of the disembodied voice he'd been conversing with, shook his head to his question.

The wave of terror and adrenaline that had gotten him out of the tree seemed to solidify and turn to lead in his body, slowing his movements, slowing his feet, grinding his thoughts to a complete stop.

She'd landed where she was bracketed in by the fire. Not moving. Not answering.

He didn't even need to ask her why she'd jumped. He knew. God help him. She'd jumped because she couldn't let herself fail, but she'd also jumped because of him. He'd gone off and she'd chased him.

If they'd stayed on the plane, there were things they could've done—aided the spotters to direct the ground crews about changes in directions of the beast. Gone back to base to pack supplies for extra runs. Mount rescues for those who needed help. She needed help.

"Ellison. Get it together." Kolinski whacked the back of his head, jarring his thoughts loose from the spiral they'd funneled into. "Did you hear what I said?"

"Get it together," Beck repeated dully, the sense of detachment from his body growing stronger with every passing second.

"I said she's up."

Beck clicked his comm and called her, twice, but got no answer. His breaths were sharp, like knives going through him sideways, and he had to work to shove words through a throat that felt almost closed. "She's up?"

"She landed hard. Looks like her comm is busted."

"Is she hurt?"

"Not sure, but she's up."

"Who are they sending after her?"

Kolinski looked at him a hard second, then shook his head. "She has a map and compass, emergency supplies in her pack. It's on her to hike out and she'll do that. It's SOP."

Not enough. He'd throw away his responsibilities to the crew and go after her at that second if he knew where she'd landed.

Kolinski seemed to see that on his face too, and thrust a saw into his hands. "You're cutting."

All he could do was nod and make his body start working again, stripping off his jumpsuit and making for the real gear. "I want every update. If she starts going the wrong direction, I'm going after her, even if it's the end of my job."

The lieutenant nodded once, then pointed to the tree-line in the southeast. "We need a wide firebreak. Cut ruthlessly."

Don't panic.

First rule of survival in a bad situation: Don't. Panic.

Lauren worked herself free from the lines of her parachute, which had wrapped around her as she'd rolled.

It wasn't on fire. She wasn't on fire. Her hands shook, but her fingers still obeyed when she found the buckles on her chute and got them open.

How had she rolled through that without catching fire? They weren't flame retardant… Felt like a miracle.

Heat baked in from three sides, causing her to

sweat badly enough for her feet to slide around in boots just a touch too big for her.

She needed to move. Her suit wasn't the kind of gear made for facing a fire. They had to jump as light as they could, carrying only meager survival packs, with the expectation they'd regroup at the dropped supplies. That's what she should be doing.

Instead, she was surrounded by fire, and had just noticed her right shoulder throbbed in a way she could only think meant damage. Her heart slammed so hard and fast it might wear out at any second. So hard she couldn't hear anything but her heart beating in her ears. Was her comm even working? Were they coming for her? Did she even want them to do that?

North looked open. She began scrambling up the only bare spot of slope she'd been able to reach with her bad drop zone. The peak wasn't far. Then she'd be able to see what she was up against. She didn't know how far the non-burning patch of earth continued. It could be that just over the rise she'd find another firewall.

What had she seen on the way down?

Fire.

Lots of freaking fire.

She'd been blinded to anything else—just the fire and her efforts to steer her chute away from it.

If she didn't get better at this job fast, she might as well quit when she got out. If she got out.

The earpiece in her ear squawked suddenly, cutting through the swishing, pounding awfulness in her ears, then nothing. No time to stop and check it, she kept going.

Gasping from some motivating cocktail of heat, effort, fear, and pain, she made it to a clear spot at the top and the downslope spread out before her, a large valley of green. Not leaping red, orange, and yellow. Not burning. The fire blanketed the south behind her, and stretched out east and west, but north was clear. For now. Who knew how fast the fire was moving?

Go north. Get out of the oven. She'd be okay.

Get to the bottom of the valley, then stop to get directions and to see if her comm could be repaired.

"You can do this. It's just a hike. A vigorous, terrifying hike. Downhill. See? That's perfect. Downhill is awesome. It'll be fast." Sometimes an internal pep talk wasn't enough. Sometimes the words needed to be said out loud to drown out that damned internal voice of criticism she was so prone to hearing. The words even made it over the pounding in her ears while the roar and crackling of fire and trees splitting she should be hearing didn't.

Probably some kind of delusion.

Halfway down the slope, when the ground became a gentler incline, she plucked the earpiece out, found the wires apparently intact, but tugged on them a little bit to test the connection anyway. Looked right. She put it back in, tugged at the base of the wires, then slapped the box a couple of times. Nothing happened. As if banging broken electronics ever fixed them.

Should she turn it off and turn it on? Pop the batteries? Lord, she didn't know how to fix things. Why didn't she know how to fix things?

More importantly, why had she jumped?

Just thinking of the leap summoned the sensation of free fall, those seconds before her chute had jerked her up clung to her, and got worse when she started berating herself for this failure. Another failure.

Why had she even gone up? She should've told them. She should've just *told* them. Confessed her error. It was an error, not made with malicious intent. Just an error that fear had exacerbated.

If she'd told them, at least then she would've scratched out of training because of her stupid application miscalculation, but at least she'd be alive for her family to give her hell over it.

Beck made it back to camp with daylight still lighting the skies, but came into an empty cabin.

Lauren wasn't back yet.

She'd had to hike out by herself because of him, and he still didn't know if she'd been retrieved or if she was still in the woods.

He slammed into the cabin, then straight on to the shower. He'd ridden a spike of terror all day, and stank of it.

There was nothing to do but keep busy. Keep busy and do the things that needed doing. Clean up. Get dinner. Get *two* dinners, so if she got back after they closed up evening chow she could still eat something. Something besides an MRE, because, God knew, those were awful.

The thought of food ration packs conjured the chemical taste he always had to fight to ignore when choking them down. But standing in the shower, he let himself consider every aspect of that fake, preservative-laden bite. It was better than the thoughts that had been consuming him since he'd seen her parachute drifting toward the flames.

Lauren burning. Fire eating through the suit she'd jumped in, turning her golden, beautiful skin to char. Her long caramel hair gone. Skin cracking.

He'd never actually seen someone burn, and he'd avoided movies with those kinds of special effects, but he knew what fire did. He knew the sound of bacon popping on the griddle. He knew what a forest looked like after a wildfire had consumed it. Even wood blistered and cracked in that kind of heat. Skin was nothing by comparison. He could picture it. Had been picturing it in ever increasing detail since he was a child, when his mind had been without the knowledge required to summon nightmarish levels of detail. Like it could now.

MREs and their cocktail of chemical flavors were heaven to think of by comparison.

Fake butter flavor.

The metallic taste of tomato sauces when the chemical heat was applied.

He made it through the shower, dried, dressed, and went on to the next task. Always the next task. He checked in with the office for word, learned she'd been picked up, sore and slightly injured. Went to get dinners.

Picked pine needles and tied them up in a cloth, getting salts ready for the soaking bath she'd probably need if she'd landed hard enough to kill her comm.

Then he sat on the front stoop of the small cabin and waited. Waited and tried to listen to the frogs singing in the woods behind.

Stopping Lauren from going up this morning when he could see how it unnerved her would've really pissed her off, but it would've been for her own good. Making her take time off now that she was injured would also be for her own good.

Was she hurt badly enough to bow out until next year? God help the man who suggested such a thing to her.

He didn't see her small frame slogging across the dark field until she was almost on him, and it took every ounce of willpower not to rush over and scoop her up, frisk her for injuries, shout at her, shake her…kiss her.

Lauren stopped in her tracks, looking at him like he was everything wrong in her life.

"Are you hurt?" he asked, trying to play it cool as he rose from the cabin steps.

In answer, she walked forward, then turned sideways to get past him and up the few steps into the cabin.

There was nothing to do but follow.

And, because he could feel big emotions weighting the air like a summer storm, he closed the door behind him.

"You didn't answer." He reached to take her shoulder to spin her and look for injuries, but at the first touch she ducked and turned, smacking his hands away. In the low light of the cabin her scowl was unmistakable.

And she was hurt, he realized dully. She was right-handed, and had smacked at him with her left hand, her right arm held close to her body.

"Let me see."

"Shut up. You left me on the plane. You jumped without me!"

"I know…" He didn't reach for her again. Not yet, but the desire still lit him and his hand hovered between them, as far from his body as it was close to hers. "Let me see your arm. How did you hurt it? Is it broken?"

"It's bruised," she grunted, and shoved at his hand again with her left hand. "You're an awful partner, you know that, right?"

"I do." He tugged his hair back from his face, trying to stretch his scalp and defuse the tension headache he'd been nursing.

"Why did you just jump like that? Why didn't you say something to me? Ask what was wrong? Maybe there was some reason I didn't jump."

Her equipment had been checked before they'd boarded the plane, that was something Kolinski had been adamant about—checking the rookies' equipment. He'd known there hadn't been anything wrong with her pack. It had been inside, and he'd seen it before they'd even gotten on the bus to go to the hangar.

"You panicked."

She flung that one good arm up and in the very next second her eyes were wet and every ounce of angry color lurking behind her dirty cheeks drained away. "I *know*!"

"It's okay. It happens…"

"No, it's not okay. It doesn't happen to people who've…been…who've…" She stopped and shook her head, then started jerking at the flight suit's zip, wrestling it down so clumsily that he felt compelled to step closer and help with that, but did it with slow, open-palmed motions that let her know he wasn't going to do anything bad, just help.

Maybe taking care of that physical stuff would let her mouth take care of whatever wanted to come out. "People who've jumped into wild-fires?"

The zipper eased down with her not jerking on it. He watched the slow descent, opening to the strong, supple body he knew he'd find beneath. She was dressed in shorts and a top, nothing too revealing, but a surge of heat still hit his middle and he had to step away, especially as her scent hit him.

"People who have jumped from a plane be-fore." She whispered the words, pulling his gaze back to hers.

Even whispered, the words jarred. "What?"

"I never jumped before," she said, a little more firmly.

"Low altitude?"

"No altitude!" Her voice started to rise again, panic coming out despite the fact that her feet were firmly on the ground now.

"Why did you say you had?"

She'd lied her way into the air?

If he'd known earlier... Holy, blessed nature, he'd have hog-tied her to keep her off the plane.

The look of unconcealed helplessness she gave him made him want to shake her again.

He hadn't known her long, not really, but he knew that she faked confidence when she didn't feel it. She'd done that this morning. And every day this week.

Right now, she was upset, scared, and either too overwhelmed to hide it or just didn't care enough to hide it anymore. Neither sounded good.

He should've figured it out by now, after all the signs today. That hint of fear at being told about the tower had made her go white. So had word they were going up. Then her inability to jump, and the god-awful landing. Landings were hard at first, and landing in a small patch of earth surrounded by fire without smashing into trees? It was a miracle she wasn't dead.

"Why the hell didn't you say something?" he asked, curling his fingers into his palms so he didn't shake her as she was already injured.

"I panicked! I panicked because I'm in totally over my head. Everything Dad said was right. I didn't mean for this to happen. I just... Things happened and everything snowballed and I didn't know how to get out of it. And now I'm done. They're going to come and ask what happened, and I'm going to have to tell them and they're

going to boot me out for lying on my application.
Before I get myself killed, or worse, get someone else killed. I should've been able to do it. I
should be able to do it. It's in my freaking DNA!
Unless it's carried on the Y chromosome, hah!"
The short, barked laugh hit like a slap. "He was
right. He was right and I'm... I should just go be
a *baker* or something."

The long self-berating babble stopped his
anger cold.

Her left hand flew all over, gesturing, ranting,
but she kept that right one to her chest.

He wasn't sure where this was going but,
knowing she dealt with sexism in regard to the
job, felt the need to point out, "I don't think being
a woman has anything to do with you screwing
this up."

"Thank you for that!" she grunted, then went
right back into her self-targeted tirade. "Actually, I guess I'm selling my aunts and grandmoth-
ers short. They weren't just people who minded
the kitchen. They were reporters. People who
talked about all the heroics the menfolk got up
to. Scrapbooks. They all made scrapbooks with
the newspaper clippings. You know half that stuff
they have on the history of the department at the
local history museum is from the Autry women.
Those fine scrapbookers."

Scrapbookers. Yep, she'd gone well past the

point where sense was going to make a dent in this.

"Are you hungry? I brought food…"

"Man, now I feel bad because it sounds like I hate scrapbooks. I don't hate scrapbooks. I love them. I loved looking at them and reading all of them. Even the ones I had to wear those weird white gloves to handle. I just didn't want to make them. I don't have that talent. Maybe I don't have this one either. I want to be doing the things, actually help people. Is it wrong to want to do the things?"

"Stop," he said softly, and to stop her prowling around stepped close enough to breathe her in again. The fire she'd come so close to had left a smoky hint to that honey and dirt he still smelled, and grounded him again in what had almost happened.

Her voice dropped as well, the fire going out of it. "Stop what?"

"Take a breath." They both needed to take a breath. "Tell me what happened."

"On my application I said I had experience because I was supposed to have gotten it by the time it became relevant. But that's not what happened. Between all the things with my family and work, I just had no extra time. I didn't get the experience I'd planned for."

"Skydiving experience isn't a requirement.

They train from the beginning, you know that. You don't move like someone without training."

"Maybe it's not a requirement for you!" Her volume went back up, but it was more like despair than anger pitching her words. "I didn't have it last time, and I didn't make it. I wanted to cover my bases. Got a trainer three times a week at the gym. Got skydiving classes and went as far as I could with them. When the application deadline came, I should've had time to make the jumps. I even had them scheduled and paid for when I filled out the application. But my schedule got blown up and time ran out and then they sorted us into different training level groups and I didn't know how to backpedal the situation without completely wrecking everything."

Despair and disgust with herself, and those beautiful eyes that searched his, as if he had any solutions. Beck did the only other thing he could think of, wrapped his arms around her and tugged enough to get her that last step to him.

She froze, stiff as an oak in his arms, and possibly stopped breathing except she whispered, "You're hugging me…"

"Yeah…" He tilted his head to the side as she tilted hers up, dirty, pink, exhausted, and in that second devoid of all the awful emotions that had been written in capital letters on her face. "You should be warned, I'm also kind of thinking of kissing you. But that would probably be a bad idea."

Bad, and not something he did anymore. He just preferred to live his life on his own, free of the mess that came with relationships. His celibacy had even become easy at this point. And yet, with this woman, he wanted to forget all the reasons it was a bad idea to get more involved.

She nodded in return, but not in the way of someone who believed, or even knew what she was agreeing to.

"I'm going to be kicked out anyway when I tell them the truth."

She lifted her ranting hand and brushed the tips of her fingers down his cheek. She wanted the kiss. And if that wasn't obvious, she stared now at his mouth like her gaze could act like a rope to pull him in closer.

It worked. Beck felt his head lowering, and her beautiful green eyes swiveled to his once more, wide and watchful until the first brush of his lips. The hand that had been a light, tender touch at his cheek slid back, hooking around his neck to pull him closer. The boldness he'd come to expect from her before tonight was nowhere to be found. She didn't demand so much as plead for a firmer embrace, deeper kisses, in the way she melted into him, and the way her tiny wanting sounds tickled his lips.

CHAPTER NINE

LAUREN HAD HEARD the old adage that confession was good for the soul but had never actually believed it. Confession meant consequences. Worse, it meant you'd failed at something, and that something was your fault. She'd done both today—had failed, and it had been her fault.

But her confession had brought a reward, a bone-melting kiss that distracted her mind and knocked the charred edges off a terrible, terrifying day. If she was smart, she wouldn't get used to it. Telling that to anyone, even this man with lips like silk, was the first brick gone in the complete dismantling of her career.

He held her close, relief pouring through her—hers, his, and built-in permission to let herself not be strong for once, to lean on him and borrow some of his strength.

He'd been worried, felt guilty, desperate. He'd cared, and his kisses were tinted with it, a shot of bitter with the sweet.

He'd had to be locked in a police cruiser to keep him from going after the fireman. Had they had to restrain him today to keep him from coming for her? Had his own actions been the lesson he'd needed to be a better team member, to not run off and abandon his team?

Was she just grasping at straws because she desperately needed a win? Maybe. But held tight against his strong frame, she let herself indulge in the fantasy that everything was fine now, and surviving was the happy ending they both needed.

His arms tightened around her waist, and she had to ease her right arm out of the space between their chests to wrap over his shoulders, needing to be closer too.

Kissing him was like an opiate. She barely felt the pain in her shoulder and the various bruises she'd yet to take inventory of. She barely felt the fear and dread of what was coming next. It was just a slow descent into honeyed warmth and blissful *nothing*. Supporting her weight in his arms, her toes lightly traced back and forth as he swayed with her, rocking away the horrible.

"Someone's here," he suddenly said against her lips, and she realized a second later she'd heard a knock at the door too.

"Kolinski." She whispered his name.

His arms relaxed slowly and she found herself

on the floor before him, unable to tear her eyes off his mouth.

His…sooty mouth.

"Go wash your mouth. He's here for me."

"He'll want to talk to me too."

She tried again, gesturing to her own mouth. "Nose to chin, you've got a sooty clown mouth thing going on."

He looked completely baffled at her and she almost grinned.

"Didn't you ever get a lipstick smear before?"

"I never wear lipstick," he said, expression too serious except for a slight lifting of the corner of his sooty mouth. Joking. He was joking.

She grinned and played along, the teasing making things better somehow. "You'd look really nice in a soft, beachy coral."

Kolinski pounded on the door again, and she stepped back, giving Beck a small shove toward the bathroom while she went to face the music.

Her right arm clamped right back to her body because the pain surged as her senses returned, she opened the door. "Come in, Lieutenant."

Kolinski only stepped in far enough to close the door behind him, and looked past her to Beck, who was drying his face.

"Who wants to tell me what happened up there?"

Beck looked at her a second, and she lifted

her good hand, ready to spill the beans, when he cut in.

"I screwed up," he announced, keeping his eyes on the lieutenant, not responding to her wide *what are you doing?* eyes. "In the past week I've become...attached to Autry. When it came to it today, I tried to get her not to jump because I hadn't ever seen her make an actual jump before and panicked about her going for the first time over a fire."

Lauren didn't have to look in a mirror or have anyone ask, she felt her mouth fall open at Beck's words.

He was taking the blame for her screwup.

He was *covering* for her. Making sure her stupid lie didn't come out. It was such a thing that could never happen, she wasn't even certain it *was* happening.

"What did you do to make her not jump?" Kolinski asked, then looked at her, which prompted her to try and close her mouth again because she didn't know what to say.

Beck clearly hadn't put any thought into this plan. He *umm*ed a couple times, then said, "Said some nasty things about her being...not ready."

"You said nasty things about her not being ready, then went ahead of her and told her not to jump?"

"Yeah."

It sounded like a lie. It was so obviously a lie. Kolinski crossed his arms and stared at Beck, then included her in his stare. It was a lot harder to lie with your mouth than with pen and paper and the shame of poor follow-through on your planning.

Beck's jaw had clamped shut. She could feel her own stunned expression like a mask on her face. Neither of them looked normal. They looked like liars.

Liars Kolinski was playing along with. "So he jumped without you and you decided to go anyway?"

"He…" She didn't want to blame him, and she really didn't want to lie anymore. They'd accept it if she said she needed more of a refresher before going back up, or if she asked to be bumped back with the rest of the rookies.

Whatever she said, she couldn't let him lie for her.

"I panicked when I saw the fire below," Lauren admitted, then added, "Beck's trying to help me now because he's my partner. And maybe because he feels bad for having jumped when I was struggling. He went ahead, it's his job, then I started feeling like a total failure and made myself go. Didn't think so much time had passed. It was my fault. He's just trying to look out for his partner now."

She didn't know what to think about that grown-attached business, so she didn't say anything about that.

Kolinski shifted his gaze from one to the other for several long, heart-stopping seconds. "If you've got a romance going on and it's screwing everything up, you should both be re-partnered."

"We don't need to be re-partnered," Lauren said quickly, shaking her head. "He was just covering."

Beck backed her up then. "It was a glitch. We both screwed up and it won't happen again. I'm trying. She's helping me…"

Kolinski nodded. "She knows?"

Beck nodded once.

The lieutenant shifted his gaze to her then. "Did you have your arm looked at?"

"I did. It's bruised."

"Not broken? Not sprained?"

She shook her head.

"Okay, then this is a warning. Formal paperwork will be in your boxes tomorrow. Get your act together. One more and you're both out."

Kolinski delivered his lovely parting words then left, and Lauren locked the door behind him.

Then she was back at Beck's side, completely unable to summon the words to ask why he'd done that, gone to bat for her, lumped his fate in with hers.

"It was my fault. Stupid. I shouldn't have jumped. I shouldn't have gone up there. I can't let you *lie* for me."

"I was trying to have your back. Share the blame." He sounded a little put out, but there was nothing to be done for it. "And it was my fault too. You were my partner and I abandoned you. We have to do better than this."

"Why was this strike two? What was strike one?" She hadn't gotten anything official in her box before.

His lips thinned again, and he grunted. "Probably the day we burned the field."

When she'd had to chase him all over. He'd earned them that strike, but they'd both earned today's.

She nodded, and when she found herself looking at his mouth again, stepped back toward the bathroom. "I need to soak this grime off. And… erm…we should…we should file that whole… kissing thing under the *Romance Leads to Re-partnering* column, and, you know, maybe don't do it. We can't afford to get distracted."

"Kolinski did look against the idea of something going on," Beck said, brow beetled in the kind of deep thinking that never led to good outcomes. "I'll get the pine needles."

She'd almost gotten the door closed when his

palm suddenly touched down and pushed it back open a bit. "After I see that arm."

"Beck…"

He shook his head. "I'm not leaving until I know how bad it is."

It sounded a lot like the kinds of words that usually ticked her off, but considering his attempt to help her with Kolinski… She sighed and unzipped the suit and eased it down to her waist, baring the simple tank top she wore beneath.

"See? Not broken."

She barely got the words out when he sucked in a sharp breath and began muttering under his breath.

"It's okay."

She didn't want to look at it, she'd seen enough of the eggplant-colored splotch earlier when the EMT had checked her over, and seeing his reaction was enough to confirm it wasn't any better.

His touch was gentle, but he didn't shy away from making her move her arm, testing her range of motion through her wincing, making sure that ball joint functioned the way it was supposed to. "It's not broken, it's bruised."

"You need a sling."

"I don't need a sling."

"You've been keeping it clamped to your chest to stabilize it because it hurts. You need a damned sling, Lauren." He scrubbed his hands over his face and paced away then back to her. "In the morning, I'll get you one from the infirmary."

It was on the tip of her tongue to deny needing a sling again, but maybe it would help things heal faster. It would certainly help his mood.

"Okay. I'll wear a sling for a couple of days until it feels better."

He turned back to her, surprise pitching his eyebrows to high, crazy angles.

"What? I can compromise."

"Okay." He nodded, hands on his hips. "Can you accept help too?"

"You just helped. I let you."

"With jumping."

She stopped, the subject shift throwing her. "What...? Which part?"

"How we can fix it." His tilted his head and the way his black eyes fixed on her said as much as his words. How *we* can fix it. Not how *you* can fix it. We.

One simple word and the weight that had been crushing her lifted, letting her stand straighter, letting her smile again.

This was it. This was what having a partner felt like. She had to look away from those deep, meaningful looks to hide the mistiness in her eyes.

"You have an idea?"

"You know you can make the jump, but you

need to practice landing." He let go of the door and nodded to her shoulder. "Don't worry about it now. A man I served with has a plane, operates a small business out of the local airport. I'll see if he'll take us up in a couple of days."

Us. The sweet ping of pleasure in her chest at the word only grew warmer as she caught up to the rest of it. He was going to *help* her, even after she'd refused to let him take the fall for her. Even after everything.

He'd already started moving again, saying something about salts. Another way he was helping.

She had to find a way to help him too, she just didn't know how.

The weekend passed for Lauren in a blur. She slept so long on Saturday Beck had come into her room to wake her up and make her go to dinner. She'd been having a dream so over-sexed she was sure he'd known. No one moaned when being woken up. That was never the appropriate reaction.

Lauren?

Moan.

Not at all humiliating. And the goofy smile? Yep. Just added to it. She might as well have moaned his name. She might *have* moaned his name.

If she had, he'd been blessedly tight-lipped about it. Just insisted she wear the sling he'd gotten for her, and not use her arm to do anything, despite him dragging her to the mess hall directly after. She'd missed breakfast and lunch, and healing bodies need protein, and blah-blah-blah.

He'd provided her with another sachet of pine needles and his tub-o-salts to put together her own soak afterward and gone to sleep outside for a reason he'd never explained, and she didn't ask about. Maybe he'd needed fresh air. Maybe he'd just wanted some distance from her so he didn't tempt her to more kissing...

God, she probably *had* moaned his name.

Sunday she'd been the one to make an escape—first shopping to lay in some supplies, then the Laundromat with her soiled *everything*, and her arm in the darned sling.

By Monday, she was feeling better, and although they still required her to be on another day of light duty—no push-ups or the tree-climbing designated for classroom work that day—she talked her way into being allowed the use of both arms. And she ran. In the morning, in the afternoon, and all without any existential emotional flare-ups. Another small miracle. Or a sign of her growth. She'd like to think so, at least.

Tuesday her week started to turn around. Beck got in touch with his marine buddy and as it was no longer *Hell Week*, they had somewhat shorter days, which left time to go up with Gavin, the pilot, for three low-altitude jumps to practice jumping and landing.

Her shoulder had done fine.

Between jumps, Beck had given pointers on how to land without breaking anything.

Wednesday they did it again.

Now, suited up and sitting in Gavin's plane, flying two counties away to a forest that had burned last week, Lauren turned to her partner-cum-trainer. "Why are we going to jump over an old burn again?"

"All new smokejumpers should see the aftermath of a forest fire."

"I was in actively burning woods. What am I supposed to be learning from that?"

"Devastation." He hadn't had them fly out this far for no reason, but she understood fire. It took a little work to not be insulted by the insinuation that she was unfamiliar with the destruction left behind, reminding herself he took fires personally. He saw fires like monsters, not natural things. Maybe *he* was the one who needed to come to the fire. Or maybe he just needed to be convinced she understood it.

If that was it, that was fine. She could deal

with that. He didn't have to help her with this, and if his conscience demanded he make sure she fully understood what she was getting into, that was okay too.

"Are we climbing higher?"

A look out the window confirmed the land was much farther away than their two previous days of jumps.

"Higher altitude means longer time steering the chute. We're going to circle the woods and land in the burned field beside them so you can learn to maneuver better. You're landing well, now you need better control in the air. You had trouble turning that first day."

"We're here, you two," Gavin called back, interrupting her complete lack of an argument.

Beck handed her a helmet. "Ear bud inside and mic embedded in the mouth area of the helmet. Use the comm. I'll instruct on the way down. Tell me when you have trouble."

A minute later, she was in the air, her chute popping as expected, with Beck somewhere behind her. He'd jumped after she had. That was now always the new rule of jumping: he always went second so he could see if she had trouble.

Beck's voice came over the headset soon after, reminding her what she was doing while simultaneously distracting her. If she'd known how intimate it would be to have his voice in her ear, or that she'd feel it in tingles down her neck, she might have argued against it. She was supposed to be focused on mastering a new skill, not tingling in fun ways.

In truth, in just a few short days her confidence in the air had reached what she'd hoped it would be before entering the training program. The next time she was called to a real jump, she'd be fine. That was because of him. Had nothing to do with the goose bumps that swept over her from a deep, sexy voice in her ear, or the way the tiny hairs on the back of her neck stood up and saluted when his breath hit the mic and her brain supplied the sensation that would've accompanied his breath were he getting steamy in her actual ear.

She had to remind herself to start circling, but as they got closer and the blackened patch of earth became bare, broken trees, her lusty feelings evaporated. Before she knew it, her feet touched down in the burned field and she skidded along with a gust of wind dragging her chute, then rolled to a proper stop when the wind died, and was glad for the helmet protecting her face.

She gathered up her spent chute and turned in time to see Beck landing across the field, then jogged to meet him. Together, they helped one another fold their spent parachutes and stuff them into the empty bags they'd always jumped with to make the walk out easier.

"Is Gavin coming to fetch us?" she asked, falling into step when Beck began leading at a good clip straight into the blackened woods.

One step into the trees and she knew why he'd insisted on coming here. No matter what she'd thought she'd known about burned forests, walking through a wood where the trees were crusted with black, blistered bark and no rustle of leaves and twigs underfoot made the back of her neck go cold.

Fire was natural. The reason it had become a problem in modern living was because of human over-expansion into wooded areas. In centuries past, forest fires had been allowed to burn themselves out, now they needed to be managed to protect people and property. Fire was natural, but in a burned forest her senses were all assaulted by the wrongness of it. It smelled bad. It looked wrong. No brush underfoot. And none of the usual forest sounds she always took for granted. Birdsong. Insects clicking or buzzing away. Fire was natural, but being in the forest afterward felt *un*natural.

Suddenly, the image of twelve-year-old Beck going to the burned-out woods where he'd lived and his mother had died was something else she couldn't leave alone.

"Was this what it was like when you went back

home after the fire?" she asked, hurrying to catch up so she didn't have to shout such a question.

Beck stopped walking. "Nature is resilient. Within two years, everything was green again."

"Not the house..." she said, even though she didn't know what the house had looked like before. It might have been fully consumed, half-consumed, or just charred outside, gutted within.

"The house half burned," he confirmed. "Inside the remains of the house and workshop, trees were growing. Grass. Weeds..."

House and workshop.

"You went inside?"

He started walking again, though this time at a slower speed. "Had to make sure she wasn't there."

Her hand flew over her mouth and she blinked away the sharp pierce of sudden tears heating her eyes as she realized that his mother's body had never been found. No words came.

Her new muteness earned a look, and he stopped walking again to pull her hand from her mouth. "You asked."

"Yeah... Just... You didn't find her, right?"

He shook his head and started walking again, still holding the hand he'd pulled from her mouth. "Why *did* you ask?"

His large, strong hand in hers made it harder to focus. Hands of a man who worked outside and manned a shovel, with calluses her own hands were starting to mirror. They fit together like puzzle pieces, square here, round there, textured. Hands that could hold a person no matter the conditions, wet or covered in soot and mud. Strength she saw inside him daily expressed in the strong grip of his hand. He didn't hold loosely, his fingers wrapped around hers tight enough to meld flesh, but not enough to hurt. Not treating her like she was delicate but like she was something worth holding on to.

God, she was going to cry again.

"You're doing all this for me, and I barely know you. Except that you're brave, and good, and you have a very sad story. I guess I just want to know."

He made some sound that let her know he'd heard, but didn't say anything until they'd reached a large, gnarly tan oak, leafless and charred, which he, strangely, patted on the way past. "What do you want to know?"

"I don't know. What was the workshop for?"

"Mom was a carpenter. Artist, actually. Sculptor. But making ornate furniture was more lucrative than sculptures. She custom-made modern replicas and new designs with old-fashioned techniques and beautiful carvings. Paid well."

His mother had been a carpenter. She'd never

actually heard those words from someone before. Father? Sure. Mother? Never.

"That's amazing. Have you ever looked for any of her work?"

"To buy back?"

"Yeah. To have it. What was her name? Did she mark her pieces?"

"Her name was Molly, and she'd mark the pieces with a brand in hidden places. I've never looked for anything, but I do have a trunk she made. It survived the fire. It's at my cabin."

The walk through the woods was probably a couple of miles, and then another mile south along a winding state route, but it flew by. Beck had said once he didn't like to talk about his mother, but in the woods, with Lauren's hand in his, he talked. Quietly. Reverently. How it was to grow up in such a quiet, isolated way. Home-schooled. Taught to tend a garden and help in the workshop. The two of them building him a treehouse he used to sleep in when it was warm enough. A life that taught a love of nature, and books, and quiet evenings looking at the stars. It sounded so idyllic she didn't want to think about what his life became after, and he'd only spoken of that enough that she knew it had involved foster care.

Soon he let go of her hand and waved to a taxi

speeding down the highway, which pulled onto the shoulder to wait for them.

Before they got in, she asked one final question. "Have you ever been to see what's become of the land now? If someone bought it, built new?"

A quick, slight tilt of his head showed his confusion. "Nothing's built there."

"You've been?"

"I still own it. There's a trust and it's paid the taxes."

He'd kept it, but he never went there.

He gestured toward the open door, and she did the only thing she could: climb in and scoot to make room.

Asking why he'd kept it but avoided going there for over a decade felt like a bridge too far, even for their new little relationship. Their friendship. Partnership. Whatever. She couldn't ask him that. Not yet.

And not for the whole ride to the nearest airstrip, where Gavin was waiting for them to fly back.

From the moment they climbed into the taxi, he was different. Quieter. She didn't need to ask the question burning through her. The words he'd pick to answer didn't really matter, the act itself was an answer. It would've been more financially smart to let the unused land go, or to build his own cabin there rather than buying new land, but he'd done neither. It was a place he couldn't let go of, but still didn't want to go to.

They went through the motions for the rest of the evening, grabbing dinner on the way back to camp, eating, talking about her and the Autry clan—exploits of her ancestors and immediate family rather than him. He'd earned an emotional rest after their walk through a burned-out, life-less landscape. But the switch in subject hadn't eased him.

As the hour grew late, she went to knock on his bedroom door and found it open, and he was pulling on a pair of sweats over a fresh set of gym clothes and a hoodie.

"Cold?"

He turned and looked, shifting the clothes for comfort before he sat and reached for clean socks.

"I'm going to go up the wooded trail. There's a tan oak I like…"

"The one you were sitting in that evening on the first run?"

He nodded, his expression too closed to read.

"You're going to go sleep in the tree?"

"It's really fine."

"I'm not worried about you falling." She was more worried about his insides than his actual body.

"No need to worry at all. I'll be there for morning PT." He zipped into his hoodie and came toward the doorway where she stood, stiff, wary, blocking his escape route. "Bring me a coffee when you come down?"

He tilted to slide through the space between her body and the door, but she still moved out of the way.

As bad an idea as she knew it was, the urge to stick beside him and get closer had grown beyond her control. Especially considering that today she understood his retreat wasn't just about maintaining distance with her, it was a reaction to something. The burned woods. Maybe her questions.

Tomorrow she might not be able to say the thing in her heart she needed to say to him.

"You know, if you ever wanted to visit your land, I would go with you."

He stopped on the way to the front door and half turned back, his expression sad but at war with something lighter. Something like hope.

It was only a second and he prowled right back to her. No more hesitation, he wrapped his arms around her waist and pulled her to him. The next instant, his warm, soft lips pressed to hers, one slow, long, tender kiss, so different from the frantic, need-filled devouring kiss he'd laid on her after her bad jump. It was just his mouth on hers, one slow, sweet press of flesh, gentle and tender, and somehow more substantial, not built on out-of-control emotions or a needed confirmation of life. Intimate. An acknowledgment of the closeness they'd forged this week.

When he lifted his head to look at her, there was no way to conceal the tears she felt stinging her eyes.

"I'm okay," he said softly, then released her and backed toward the door. "Don't forget my coffee. You know I'm useless without it in the morning."

Not true. Words meant to normalize what was so far from normal, but she still felt herself going along with it, nodding and watching as he slipped out the front and closed the door behind him.

CHAPTER TEN

ANYTIME BECK NEEDED to find peace, he went to the woods. It always worked, at least enough to still whatever had unsettled him or prompted extreme inner tension.

When he'd been able to fall asleep in the crook of the tree, he'd expected that the off-feeling he'd been having would be better in the morning. It wasn't. It still twisted at his insides.

His offer to help Laura gain the jump experience she'd needed hadn't been as altruistic as she'd thought. Sure, he'd wanted to help her, but he'd also expected that once satisfied she could handle herself. However, the fear that had set up house in his guts when she'd been stranded and had needed to hike out of a wildfire alone hadn't dissolved. It was still there.

The prospect of her going back up into the air and to another fire filled him with the kind of anxiety he'd have thought would be reserved for someone actively in danger, not just someone in possible future danger.

Lauren wasn't just someone. She was the only person he'd actually allowed to get close since Mom had died, and even the idea she could die the same way brought the most horrific visuals to his mind.

He'd tried to fake normal with her all day, through the long looks and the faint worry line that kept appearing between her brows. Hadn't pulled it off, but didn't know what to say about it.

The last run of afternoon PT finished and they were both still catching their breath when Treadwell surprised everyone by slowly walking onto the field.

"He looks better," Lauren said quietly, a safe subject, one he could talk about. "Still pale, but not that terrible gray."

Unlike the rest of the group, they hung back and let the mob gather to welcome the chief. He wasn't a man to suffer fawning, and the shrill whistle he loosed through tight lips both cut through the din and summoned Beck and Lauren at the same time.

"I'm not back," he announced first. "Call just came in for assistance from a local station with a big fire at an apartment complex. It's bordered by woods and they need help. Anyone up for it, go now."

He finished with directions by pointing toward

the main building, then turned to slowly walk back in that direction.

Beck needed only a glance at Lauren to know she was going. Her gaze connected with his, and they turned in unison to jog for the main building. They were a team now, and he had no choice about letting her face any fires alone. In the future, when she was assigned to a team, that would change—something he didn't want to think about. Right now, he only knew that, no matter how skilled she might be, she'd be safer at his side than anyone else's.

Half an hour later, they were both in full gear at the site and being directed to the last building at the back, which was supposed to have been evacuated but had finally caught fire and needed a final sweep.

Others followed with hoses and began the attack.

"Upstairs down," she said. "Keep to the cement breezeways as much as possible. These buildings are built with metal skeletons. If the floor looks iffy, stick to the joists."

Over what was probably only ten or fifteen minutes, they scouted the third floor of the building, found nothing, and moved down to the second.

She moved quickly, assessing everything and gesturing him off on different paths he might not have traveled without her. Contrary to how he always felt in a wildfire, really contrary to how he'd felt in the hours she'd outrun one alone, even contrary to knowing structure fires were statistically more dangerous, Beck didn't feel that spike of chained-up terror in his chest. Until the back of the second floor, when he suddenly did.

It took him a heart-squeezing to realize what his body had reacted to.

Screams. He'd heard a woman screaming.

And behind it a baby's cries.

One look at Lauren confirmed she'd heard it too, and had flipped up the visor on her helmet so she could hear more clearly, and it was there in the whiteness around her mouth.

Woman and child, trapped behind a burning doorway, and who knew what else.

"Is there another way?" he asked, praying she had an idea that hadn't come to him. All the apartments had balconies, but getting in through a balcony would require leaving, getting a ladder, climbing in—time they didn't have.

She flipped down the visor and gestured to the stairs and took them at a run, and he followed. In building fires, she was definitely the more experienced, and he'd take whatever wisdom that experience brought. A moment later, they were on the ground below a balcony, and she'd thrown down all the equipment except for her protective clothing.

"I'm going to climb, and you're going to lift me."

"Alone?"

"Do you have a better idea?"

He gaped for only a second, tempted to tell her to wait. To tell her if they didn't know she could go in safely, she shouldn't go—things she'd said to him before, but which he knew neither one of them believed at that moment. Woman. Baby. It was worth the risk.

Sweat that had been pouring off him below the gear ran like ice water down his spine, but he linked his fingers to offer her a step up. "Use the wall to steady yourself as I lift, and when you're high enough, grab the balustrade."

If she could reach it. If he could lift her high enough.

Climbing would require a sure grip, so she pulled the bulky gloves off and stashed them in the pockets of her jacket, then stepped into his hand.

A moment later, he'd heaved her up to the height of his shoulder. She tested the heat of the wrought-iron bars framing the balcony, then grabbed hold and began to lift herself, allow-ing them to share the burden as he extended his arms up over his head and she was high enough to reach one foot up to the balcony and climb.

In less than a minute she was over the bar, had her gloves on again and peeked into the sliding glass door. The locked door.

"Axe," she called down to him, then leaned over to catch it as he tossed it up.

That was the last word she said to him before he heard shattering glass, and then he was running, around to the front again to call for a ladder and crew. It couldn't have been longer than seconds, but time slowed, seemed like hours before his shouting was heard and he finally saw men with a ladder running for him, leaving him free to barrel back around to the balcony.

By the time they got back there, she'd returned and was leaning over the railing, a screaming toddler wrapped in her jacket, his face out in the air.

"He's okay. Needs oxygen. I need your help with the mother."

Beck stepped back for the men to place the ladder, then pushed through, climbing fast to reach for the child. He passed the terrified toddler off to the next pair of hands, then hammered up the ladder and over the rail while she buckled her jacket again.

One look back into the burning apartment explained why she'd had the baby inside her coat—

the living room was a wall of flames. They were going to have to run through.

She flipped her visor down again, put her gloves back on, pointed, and repeated her earlier advice. "Stay on the joists."

It only took seconds for her to explain the distance between floor joists, then she was gone. He followed.

Once inside, even in a room on fire, the consuming fear he expected didn't come. The fire that surrounded them in that building wasn't a monster. It was a thing. It was her conquering the deep end of the pool, no one there to stop her. Not something plotting to hurt this family, just a sad, unfortunate event.

"Mrs. Rhodes," she called, visor up again, and moved around a recliner to the floor where the woman was sprawled.

The first sight of her almost took Beck's breath. The pink plaid pajamas she wore were singed on the top and almost entirely missing on the bottom, melted into her legs or consumed by the fire.

Her legs…

"We can't carry her out like that. She needs protection…"

"I have the fire blanket." Lauren was already shaking it out, but the bathroom was just right there…

Beck stepped in and yanked open the closet

inside to fish out a couple of towels, which he tossed into the bathtub, and turned on the cold water.

"Beck?"

"One minute," he called, moving the towels under the fully open faucet until they were saturated, then carrying both out. "Here. Lay these over the burns to keep them from getting heated when we run through."

Lauren had already spread the fire blanket on the floor and eased Mrs. Rhodes onto it, but took one of the towels Beck offered and laid it over the leg that had taken the worst of it. The skin was gone in some places, and bubbled up to terrible blisters in others.

"I have flu," the woman sobbed, shaking her head. "I was asleep. I... The alarms..."

"It's okay. We're going to get you out."

"My son..."

"He's scared, but he's fine." Lauren spoke firmly, projecting confidence Beck didn't feel. Couldn't feel. Not while seeing those burns... "We're going to take you to him now, okay?"

Mrs. Rhodes nodded, and since they had her covered in the wet towels, Beck flipped his visor down then flipped Lauren's down as well before bending to wrap the poor woman in the blanket so they could pick her up and make a run for it.

In nothing less than a joist-to-joist sprint, they

made it back through the fire and out onto the balcony, then down the ladder and on to the ambulances.

The fire alarms had woken the woman, and she'd run through fire to her son. She hadn't hesitated. No shoes, no protection, and she had gone for her son.

The story stuck to him, along with the way she'd sobbed her apologies to them, to the baby who didn't know what his mother had done to save him. The kind of love that allowed such sacrifice shouldn't hurt to witness, but even well outside the heat of the fire it burned straight through him.

Lauren handled all communication, getting new orders once their building was clear, and waved for him to follow. She'd already started moving to another building, setting a pace he'd fight to keep up with the rest of the evening.

They worked for hours, first making sweeps and then manning the hoses, and she'd never lost a drop of that energy. At the site or inside burning buildings, there was no hint of the hesitation he'd seen when they'd been digging or even at camp. She was confident and certain of herself, every bit the force of nature they fought, and he had to wonder if she'd joined the smokejumpers because she wanted to do the job or because she thought it would finally give her the validity in the eyes of her family.

This seemed to be what she was made for. If he was honest, he craved this *for her.* He needed this woman in his life, whatever way she'd take him, even after training ended. So he'd just have to accept her on the crew, battling wildfires, because he had no choice.

Unless she changed her mind.

"I know you're happy to have been able to help them, but I'm just not feeling celebratory," Beck said, driving them back from the fire in his faithful pickup, hands gripping the wheel and that scowl she saw so often on his face magnified by his surly profile.

Was that anger? "How *are* you feeling?"

The more they talked about things, the less she had to badger him into putting his thoughts into words. At that moment, she only had to ask and he admitted, "Can't stop thinking about what life's going to be like for them. There's no scenario here that has a happy ending."

"What do you mean? She could live, that's a happy ending."

"She could. I hope she does. But you saw the extent of her burns. They're not going to heal easily. If they heal at all, it means a lifetime of debilitating scars."

"Right, a *lifetime*. Are you saying it would be better if she'd died?"

"Of course not," he bit out, not taking his gaze from the road. It wasn't a long drive, and he'd managed to survive most of it with her blathering on in that verbal decompressing way she had of thinking through events with her mouth.

They pulled into the camp's lot and he exited the truck, leaving her to follow in his wake.

She held her tongue until they were back inside the cabin, where no one would overhear.

"Tell me what you mean, then. Because I have rolled your words around in my head at least twenty times since we parked, but it still sounds to me like you think her death would have been better."

"You're twisting what I said. That baby's too young to understand now, but once he grows up, even if she survives, he's going to think of what happened to her every time he looks at her. Every time he sees those scars, he's going to know she got them because of him. If she dies, he'll know it's because of him. There is no happy ending. There is only life or death."

"It won't matter to him knowing how much she loves him?" she said, recalling their conversation on the bus. It hadn't gotten through as much as she'd hoped it had.

He did look at her then, standing in the cabin,

hands rolling at the wrist from the tension she could see biting through his peace. "What he'll know is if he hadn't been there, she could've run the other way."

It always came back to that. To this notion he'd caused his mother's death somehow.

"Is that what you think about your mom?" she asked, unable to keep her voice level. "You think if you hadn't been born, they would've saved her? Or if *she'd* gone first, something no good mother would ever do, she would've *ever* been the same if she'd lost you?"

"If I hadn't been born, there would've been time to save her, yes." He conveniently ignored her other question, because there was no way around it—or the concept just shut him down. It seemed to have done so on the bus.

Which was fine. He wasn't ready to deal so she'd fight him on the front he offered. "If I hadn't been born, my mother might not have died of breast cancer. Pregnancy hormones very likely triggered her cancer. Is it my fault she died?"

"That's health stuff. It's different."

"It's exactly the same. You're saying if you were never born, your mother could still be alive. If I was never born, my mother could still be alive. So, answer me. Is it my fault she's dead?"

"No," he said softly, then thumped onto the small, lumpy sofa, head in his hands. "Do we have to talk about this? We worked together well. We got the job done. You wanted to know what I was thinking. I told you. Why does it have to be a fight?"

"It's only a fight when you're thinking things that make no sense." But maybe he needed to hear these things said out loud to see that. He was talking to her now, and, as angry as his words made her, shutting them down wasn't going to help him. "Am I not supposed to try and talk you out of thinking this way? Just let you say these things that you know are wrong?"

"I don't know they're wrong. They're wrong in your head, you weren't there."

She couldn't contain the breath that rushed out of her, and she suddenly couldn't keep standing either. Two steps, and she sat beside him. "You're right, I wasn't there. So, tell me what you want me to do."

His laugh was mirthless, and he leaned back, laying his head on the back of the sofa so he could stare at the ceiling. "You don't want to know what I want you to do."

The words would've sounded depressed but for the undercurrent of bitter amusement.

She didn't want to know?

Suddenly, she knew she *did* want to know. And, was pretty sure she knew already.

He didn't want help working through this. He wanted help forgetting about it.

She stared at his profile—strong jaw, angular cheekbones, long eyelashes entirely wasted on a man—then let her gaze track down over his shoulders, chest, arms with enough definition the muscle always looked flexed one way or another.

He was a sight, one she enjoyed looking at.

Having an unreasonable voice on eternal loop in her head got exhausting, and hers had just broadcast the ways she wasn't good enough. His blamed him for the death of his mother. She couldn't shut hers up, and she didn't even have to wonder if he could his.

Tonight was too fresh a reminder of his loss, and even if she didn't think the memory was ever far from his mind, she wanted to push it out. Wanted him to forget, at least for a little while. With her.

"Tell me," she said softly.

He didn't answer, but his breathing picked up.

"Tell me," she said again, then reached over and brushed the backs of her fingers over his chiseled cheek.

He opened his eyes then and turned his head to look at her. "You're playing with fire, Autry."

Her skin heated just from the way he looked at her and she couldn't help teasing. "Am I? It's only a force of nature."

"So am I," he said, reaching for her. He picked her up for the second time today, this time pulling her onto him, not pushing her away. He guided her legs to either side of his hips so she straddled him, chest to chest.

She didn't wait for him to kiss her, just wrapped her arms around his neck to pull his mouth to hers. This mouth that could say such terrible things to himself was still heady and bewitching against hers.

Large hands slid up and down her body, seeking, squeezing, tugging, palming her butt to grind her against him, tight enough she could feel every inch of his firm flesh against her. But his mouth claimed more—demanding and thorough, he might as well have been kissing every inch of her body, she felt it sparking and sizzling everywhere. Pleasure-seeking exploration that only took a moment to rocket into something needier.

There was some roughly handled material, a bra that might never fasten again, and him rolling onto the couch with her, pinning her beneath his big body, then kissing his way down every inch he wrestled free of fabric. Sucking, licking, dragging his teeth along her slender curves.

She'd meant to touch and please, but he didn't hold still long enough for her to get her mouth anywhere near him. His curling black hair tickled the plane of her belly as he continued lower, not stopping until he had one of her legs over his shoulder and her staring, dazed, down at him.

"If you don't want this, say it now, please."

"Bed." One word, the only word she could muster, loath as she was to interrupt his intentions. The next she knew, he'd picked her up and whisked her to the bedroom, never pulling his eyes from her face.

Despite telling herself it would be foolish to get involved with him, she'd become involved. She wanted to become more involved.

Seeing him tonight, the fear in him for her, for the people who needed them, the dark emotions that swam over him that he pushed aside to do the best he could for everyone. She'd be lying if she tried to pretend she didn't want it to continue, to see what they could become together. She'd be lying if she tried to pretend she didn't care in a way she knew wouldn't ever diminish, even if she didn't want to put a word to it.

That feeling had only grown stronger, and had ruined her from that first, secret jump he'd arranged. She'd be lying if she didn't admit she'd known it would come to this since that following weekend, when, in a moment of honesty while in town, she'd bought condoms despite her declarations otherwise.

Beck laid her down on the bed, but didn't join her. There was no seduction in the way he pulled and yanked at his own clothes, but the way his dark eyes roamed over her would stay with her forever. Appreciative, obsessed, soaked with enough want to leave his movements a little mindless. As soon as he'd stripped away anything that could separate them, he stretched out on the bed with her, and found her mouth again.

She loved the heat and demand in his kisses. The way he couldn't seem to get close enough to her, his hands constantly moving, his mouth always wandering, only to lunge back to hers again, as if he couldn't go long without her kisses. She loved that it wasn't practiced or smooth. Outside that room, in their lives, they were both so in control, their bodies obeying when forced through the daily punishment that was their profession, but together, seeking only to fit together, they were both clumsy and uncoordinated, drunk on sensation and need.

With them finally skin to skin, every bit of physical control left. She barely remembered the protection in her bedside table, and it took three tries to babble some semblance of the words out. By the time she managed to get the drawer open, she'd knocked the table around so hard the lamp had fallen. Actually getting it on him required complete cessation of all touching.

He stood and staggered several feet from the bed, gasping and trembling, desperate and tear-ing at the foil with his teeth. It was only half rolled down when he was back on her and thrusting the thick length deep, face hovering above hers, eyes locked as he began to move. Under the ripples and spasms of pleasure his body wrought on hers, there was a connection that left her raw. Intense and overwhelming, the unavoidable truth she saw in his eyes crashed over her.

Avoiding the word didn't change the feeling. She loved this man, every broken part of him, from the support he gave to the infuriating distance he threw up inexplicably; from the fierce heart that would risk everything to save someone, to the still-wounded little boy she caught in glimpses. Brave and a little crazy, but wasn't she too?

Beck so rarely indulged physical needs he'd either forgotten how it felt to be wrapped up in a woman, or had never been so thoroughly wrapped up before this woman. So wrapped up, nothing else mattered. The whole world could be turning to ash and soot, and he'd still want another hour with her, another minute. There was nothing else. Just her and him, no past to haunt them, no future holding bounty or punishment, nothing but right now, right here. The way she gripped him. The heat of her. His name sighed, whispered, pled. Her beautiful eyes, watching him, holding him, seeing him.

He was as shocked and gutted by the bonds he felt weaving around them both as by the pleasure of her touch, by his own urgency—moving too fast, too hard, too driven by primitive needs he could no more control than the weather.

He didn't know how long he'd been there, locked with her, moving in her, taking and giving, only that it wasn't long enough. Her strong, silken body had already tightened past the point of no return, and he saw it in her eyes. No shielding, no hiding, no bolstering of her confidence. Her kind, loving heart shone in her eyes, and she let him see everything, the depth of her feeling for him, and how much he could hurt her if he wasn't careful.

When her climax hit, her eyes took on an unfocused quality that wavered with every quaking pulse of her orgasm, taking him with her.

By the time the madness passed, his strength was gone. He could do nothing but lie against her, his head on her breasts.

He was vaguely aware of her brushing his hair back from his face, and then nothing—the emptying he'd been after since that terrible day last season when it had all gone wrong.

All he knew was that he couldn't lose her.

CHAPTER ELEVEN

"WHAT ARE WE going to do when training is up?"

Beck hadn't fully opened his eyes yet, and she patted his shoulders and asked again.

"I don't know." Still too spent to do much more than slide off her and up the bed so he could pull her to him rather than smashing her into the mattress. "Somewhere. Can't make real plans when we don't know where you'll be stationed."

"Or if we'll make it through training without another strike." She settled her head on his chest, but there was enough tension in her shoulders to show the possibility of a third strike weighed on her.

He just didn't know if it should. She might be going all in on a life she wouldn't have even chosen if she'd been allowed to find peace and acceptance in her fire station.

It was still too early to start that conversation, but he had to say something. "Do you want to go to breakfast or sleep more?"

It was Saturday, they could lie in bed all day with the door closed and no one could say anything to them, though they might start a few rumors.

"Maybe one of us should go get breakfast so we have strength later."

"Later?"

She pulled from his arms and eased out of bed, moving somewhat stiffly. "For all the sex I'm planning to demand."

Even in the face of her moving like she was sore, he smiled. An easy smile, unfamiliar as that was. "Are you stiff because of all the sex *I* demanded, or the day before that?"

"Pretty sure the day before. Fire on top of all-day calisthenics." She dug clothes from the bureau. "I'll get breakfast. You'll get dinner."

"And lunch?"

"I'll get extra breakfast, because between the demanding sex, there will be more sleep and I'm not sure that leaves time for three cafeteria runs."

"We also need to make time to talk about something."

She froze, pants pulled half-up, eyes wide. "What is it?"

From playful to fearful just because he wanted to talk?

"Really?" He pushed onto his elbows. "After everything, after planning the day in bed, you think I want to have a *breakup* talk? Or a *this meant nothing to me* talk?"

She pulled her pants the rest of the way up, but now moved with less energy.

"Well?"

She shrugged in a helpless but disgusted-with-herself way. "Maybe. Before you said that."

He dragged himself up from the bed and didn't stop until he had her sweet face in his hands and shared a long, promise-filled kiss. "How about now?"

"Pretty much not now, but curious." Sparkling eyes, pressing closer, her voice slid to seduction.

Almost as eager to get back to bed as he was.

"I can do without breakfast."

"Well, I can't." She kissed the center of his chest, then pulled away to finish dressing. "I'll hurry, though."

Fifteen minutes later, she climbed back into bed with the food and a caddy of coffee, and kicked off her shoes. "Spill it."

"Don't want to eat first?"

"You said it wasn't bad."

"I said it wasn't a breakup talk, but you might still get mad."

A grunt answered him, and she shoved a breakfast sandwich at him. "Talk fast."

With last night's fire in his mind, and how

she'd moved through it, he said, "I'm wondering if you really want to be a smokejumper."

Beck's words should've sounded like a question but rang in her head like a final statement. A statement built to make her hackles rise.

"Why else would I be doing this?"

He didn't answer for a very long time, no doubt formulating a follow-up statement-question.

Don't get mad yet. She had to mentally say the words to herself. Maybe he had some other reason for asking than criticism, but she'd heard no implication she couldn't do it. "I want to be here."

"I know you do," he agreed, speaking slowly—as he usually did. "But do you want the job afterward?"

"That's a weird thing to ask."

"Play along?" he asked, and were it not for the concern she saw in his eyes, she might have said no.

"I'm trying…"

He set his sandwich aside, and tugged the hem of her shirt up so she had to transfer the sandwich to get it off. "Let's say you've just had the best day at work ever."

"Okay."

"What happened?"

She shrugged. "A fire?"

There went her bra. He moved on to her shorts. "Close your eyes. Tell me where the fire was."

Being undressed while she was eating and being questioned by her lover about her career path meant at least thirty different sensations overloading her senses, not counting the knot of agitation that came from being questioned. The man spoke so infrequently she couldn't discount anything he said as flippant—he didn't do impulsive conversations, didn't think *as* the words came out. He thought, probably for a long time, before deciding to speak.

She closed her eyes.

"Picture your most exhilarating day on the job," he prompted again.

Not the easiest request. She laid the sandwich aside and concentrated.

He gave her a minute. "Tell me where you are."

Where was she?

The picture should be a wildfire. A mountain, like that one bad jump. Or even working as a spotter from one of the planes, but that wasn't what formed in her mind.

He didn't prompt again, just left her to it as she worked through her own thoughts.

"House."

Not usually a word that would make someone sad, but she felt the good feelings she'd been riding since last night float away.

"Are you saving someone?"

She nodded, then opened her eyes, trying to ignore the rotten hollow feeling in her belly.

"This doesn't mean anything." Even if she felt the weight of it squashing her insides. "I've been programmed to think like that since I was little. It's a remnant."

Suddenly, she didn't want to play along anymore. And she *really* didn't want to tell him she'd decided she had to come clean to Treadwell, despite having worked to get the experience she'd been lacking. At some point, probably after she finished training and they were more inclined to be forgiving. When it couldn't become her third strike.

"Do you want to know my best day?" The question came softly, as if he knew he'd just set her internal compass spinning and felt guilty.

Hearing anything about him was a salve to the new cycle of self-criticism she teetered on the edge of. She nodded.

"During the fire season, my best day is doing what we did the day of Treadwell's heart attack."

"Helping someone you care about?"

"No." He shook his head. "Burning and digging. Figuring out how to beat the fire, how to control it. I don't enjoy going into the blazes. I hate it. It's part of the job, so I do it. But my best day? Carving that line in the earth. Protecting the land behind you, the homes, the families, the wilderness, the animals. Being the barrier between. That's my best day."

Not what she pictured at all when she thought of fighting fires. Digging felt like busywork, even if she knew it wasn't.

"You hated going into the fire last night," she said again, thinking out loud. "Even before we found them."

His actions hadn't been as sure as they normally were. He'd deferred to her there, but in the field always stormed ahead and left others to follow, or not. He didn't want anyone to suffer, not people, not animals, but he didn't get joy out of the rescue, because it meant someone had to suffer first, and suffer later.

"Yes," he admitted, and opened his mouth to say more, but that damned siren blasted again, like last Saturday all over again.

They reached the field ahead of the others, Beck's question still ringing in her head.

It was early enough that to the west the sky still faded into night. Lamps dotting the field provided enough light to see, not that she was paying much attention yet.

What if Beck was right? What if she'd only come here out of some juvenile rebellion?

She gave herself a mental shake.

Focus. Something was going on. No time to be self-absorbed. Siren meant emergency, the right mind-set was preparation.

And yet? She couldn't shake it. It was *only* her future. It was *only* what she'd been working toward for two years. Everything she'd thought she wanted, right up until he'd asked that stinking question.

Sure, she'd had some unease after bungling that first jump, but they'd worked on that. Knowing what to do next in the field wasn't instinct yet, and she definitely gave herself regular hell over even slight mistakes about anything, but she'd learn.

She'd always heard about her failures from her father, her self-criticism was worse than his. It drove her to fight for perfection. And she learned from that, just as she'd learn now.

"Kolinski," Beck said quietly at her side, jerking her from her thoughts. She turned in time to see the lieutenant jogging in from the admin buildings.

Seeing them, Kolinski snapped and pointed to the mess hall. "You two, we're taking more people out today."

"What's going on?"

"Lightning storm up north. Three separate fires started and not enough rain to put a damper on it. Biggest cut across the border to Nevada, and it's racing up the Donner trail toward Tahoe."

"The whole wagon train in the olden days where they ate each other?" Lauren asked, because for some reason that was the part that stuck out to her. That and the ruggedness of the terrain.

Kolinski and Beck looked at her strangely and her brain caught up.

"And, of course, the *lake*, where people vacation. Ringed by forests. Needing protection. Right. I'm with you."

"Because of the unseasonably warm spring, we have more people camping and exploring than usual."

"Families?" Beck interrupted, alarm in his voice—already convinced of the worst-case scenario. Not simply preparing for it, but sucked back to that dark place he'd been last night.

Kolinski seemed to pick up on it too, and nodded slowly. "Anything's possible. The storm was violent and sudden, and sparked separate locations. It's a big area."

Lauren tapped Beck's arm to get his attention, and jerked her head toward the main hall.

Kolinski left to inform others as they arrived.

"Does he mean more digging or jumping?" she asked, as much to pull his head back to the job as to know.

"Both," he answered.

Something in his voice made the hairs on the back of her neck stand up. Or maybe it was the lack of words. He'd become more talkative this week. And *Both* was back to one-word answers.

With how much she understood he hated fires, she didn't even wonder what it meant.

Twenty minutes later, Beck sat behind the wheel of his truck, driving them both to the airport. They'd eaten quickly, dressed in flight suits, and he'd somehow talked her into driving there with him instead of going on the bus. Not just because he needed to get her alone, but she'd need transportation back to camp if he could get her to agree to his request.

"You're quiet." She unfastened her seat belt and slid closer, then buckled back in.

"Preoccupied," he answered.

They were a good fifteen minutes ahead of the bus—corralling more people took longer, thankfully.

"Worried about the fire?" she asked, hesitation in her voice saying that no matter how close they'd gotten, she still felt the need to tread lightly after their interrupted conversation, even if she still wanted to be closer.

He'd intended on getting to the airport before picking another fight, but dodging wouldn't win him any points.

"Trying to figure out how to talk you out of going up."

She stiffened beside him, and even with his eyes on the road he could feel her stare.

"Bet you regret getting closer now."

"Bet you're right," she grumped, then unbuckled and slid her rear right back to her original seat. "All that talk was about making me quit? You said I'm ready, that I'm doing great. What's going on?"

"You *are* doing great." He turned down the access road to the airport.

"Then what? Did I do something at the scene last night to make you think I'm not capable?"

If only he'd had time to build an argument, but they'd only known about this less than half an hour, and most of that time he'd spent arguing with himself over whether or not he should even try to stop her today. "Let me get us there. The conversation deserves all my attention, not what I can spare while driving."

She didn't say anything else, but he could feel tension rolling off her.

Three quick turns, a couple thousand miles of access roads to the hangar, where he parked.

She didn't wait for him to get going, it was practically a miracle she'd waited as long as she had. "So?"

"When we were in the apartment last night,

you were amazing." Beck turned in the seat to better see her. "You have a feel for structure fires I don't have. You know how it acts, the safest paths, and you were fearless. I was very proud of you."

"None of that adds up to *don't jump*." She unfastened her seat belt and turned slightly toward him, though her hand rested on the door handle. "You think I do a great job *and* shouldn't do it?"

Yes, it sounded stupid. He couldn't argue that. All he could do was try to explain.

"I wasn't afraid for you in the fire last night. That fire was dangerous, people were hurt, it was upsetting, but I wasn't afraid *for you* in that fire."

"But you are afraid for me with a fire that's out in the open?" she asked. "Not jumping or landing, you're afraid of me being at a fire on the land?"

"You asked me how I see fire. I thought I'd answered, but I was wrong. I don't see all fire the same. The monster waiting to take away the people I love? It's wildfire. I know it's irrational, structure fires are a thousand times more deadly, but they don't *feel* the same. They feel—"

"Like *things*?" she interrupted.

He nodded, then took a chance and reached for her hand. Although her fingers were stiff, tense, she didn't pull away. She splayed her fingers, let them slide together, and carefully flexed them to fit his. "You have to tell me the truth. Are you trying keep me from joining? Because that's not going to happen. Even if you don't want me here."

"I'm not thinking past today, but I think you might be in denial. Honestly, I'd feel better if you just joined another station instead of going back to be under your dad's thumb, but that's not what this is about. I only know that if we're both on the mountain today, I'll focus on you more than the fire, which does make me more dangerous to everyone else."

"Why?"

"Because something could happen! I know it's illogical. I'm admitting it's illogical. I know it's *stupid* to think you're worse off fighting a forest fire than in a building, but it's not something I can control. Maybe I *am* too emotional about this, but the idea… I've been seeing it in my mind over and over again. Of you being caught. Of you burning. It's… I can't have you there."

She drew a breath, a slow, stay-calm, deep breath, as if he didn't know how much his request would grate on her. To her credit, despite the frustration bubbling there, barely controlled in her voice, she still didn't pull her hand away.

"This is going to be my job. It took me two years to get here. And they *need* people today. You heard Kolinski say there may be people out there. They wouldn't be pulling in rookies if it wasn't going very badly, if they weren't fighting on too many fronts."

"I know."

"I'm not done," she said. "Just trying to be very deliberate with my word choices."

He nodded, giving her hand a squeeze, and stretched across that middle space where she'd briefly been sitting.

"If you're planning on going, then you're being unfair to me. They need bodies, but I'm not going to pull my body out of this if *you* don't also. You're my partner. I don't care if this is voluntary and not going to count against us if you go and I don't. If you bow out, I will too. That's the compromise I'm willing to make. If you stay, I stay. We can try to work on this thing that's hurting you together. But if you go, I'm going."

"And if I said I love you? If I said I love you and I'm… I'm desperate?"

She pulled her hand free. "If you say you love me to make me stay, I'm going to say you're treating me like my father and brothers do. I gave you a fair compromise. If you're not willing to take it, then it's not about you being afraid of the wildfire. It's about you not respecting that I can handle myself, and that's really not okay."

"I have to go…"

"You don't have to go. You're a rookie right now. You're volunteering."

"Not that. I mean… If I don't go…there won't be anyone there to… If Kolinski or the other captains have to make that decision that it's not worth risking one life to save a life, I can make that decision for myself."

She jerked the door of the truck open and climbed out. "You either trust them or you don't."

"I trust them, but they have different responsibilities than I do." He climbed out too, and stopped her from storming into the hangar by grabbing her elbow. "I'm putting the keys in the back bumper. So you can drive back to camp if you—"

"That's why you wanted to drive? So I could drive back when I meekly accepted your demand to not go?" She jerked her elbow from his hand and launched forward, shoving him back. "And you're still talking like your life is expendable!"

The bus rolled into the area and Lauren stepped back, shaking her head and muttering to herself as she stalked inside.

CHAPTER TWELVE

IT HAPPENED MORE often than Lauren would like to admit, where she got this angry after being love-manipulated.

Her family did it.

Troy had done it.

And now Beck. Beck, the one who was supposed to be different. Beck, the one who had *helped* her overcome the major obstacle to her making the team.

Beck, who apparently still thought *he* was expendable.

She rounded the open doors and inside the hangar sat the plane and a ton of parachute packs, ready to be put on.

So do that. Give her hands something to do besides punch him, because, as violent as she generally wasn't, it crackled in the back of her head. One cranial lightning strike after another, composed of the words she wanted to shout at him.

She grabbed the first chute, and he stepped

up beside her, scowling as he went about suiting up as well.

"You know, my family manipulates me that way. *'If you love me, Lauren, you'll find another job.'*"

"I'm not doing that."

"The hell you're not. This is brand-new, this is the first jump after…" She stopped, realizing her voice had risen and even if they were alone, she didn't want to be shouting about her sex life anywhere they could be overheard. "You love me? Tell me then, how would you feel if I was the one telling you that I was ready to run into an unsurvivable fire for any living creature. Tell me how I'm supposed to feel when you have this outlook."

"Are you saying you love me too?"

"Yeah, but you're a jerk and I'm not sure you deserve me loving you and worrying about you. Your worry isn't worth more than mine. The difference is that I'm willing to trust you. Which is kind of *stupid* considering I'm not the one who keeps saying that I'll take almost certain death on the tiny little chance that I could save a dog— even as someone who loves dogs, as I do. So, really, if anyone should stay on the ground, it's you."

"I know that."

"So stay. Stay and I'll stay, and we'll figure something out."

"There is no way out of this!" His voice went up then. "You think me going to talk to a counselor is going to magically make me okay with someone dying if I could save them?"

"You *can't* save everyone, Beck! You just *can't*. There are no-win situations. They're things that exist, and if you can't see that, you shouldn't be going out there."

The others began piling into the hangar, effectively shutting down their fight but doing nothing to shake the helpless feeling from her shoulders.

She checked the straps, making sure they were buckled right and tight enough, and grabbed another snack from nearby stashes so she'd have the energy needed for this, while Kolinski began checking gear before letting anyone onto the plane. Beck edged up to her and made a show of checking her buckles. "Tell me what I'm supposed to do."

"There are people around."

"So tell me quietly."

"Damn it, Ellison," she muttered. "You're supposed to hold yourself to the same standard you hold me to. It's not rocket science. But you hold yourself to the *I'm expendable* standard, and hold me to the *fragile flower* standard."

"I don't hold you to the *fragile flower* standard. And you know, if you were honest on your application, you wouldn't be jumping right now anyway."

That sounded...very much like a threat. Despite the heat roiling through her, a cold wave swept down her spine.

Escalating further would make this go exactly the wrong way for her.

"We'll talk about this later. The line's shortening."

She scooted that way, but he cut in front of her.

Probably so she could still back out. God, how did she keep getting these meatheads who thought so little of her capabilities?

He moved forward and upon reaching the lieutenant stopped and looked at her pointedly.

His body swayed lightly as the straps were checked, and when Kolinski cleared him, he didn't step onto the stairs up.

He kept looking at her. Not just looking, his gaze bored into her with so much anger it bordered on something darker.

"What are you waiting for?" Kolinski asked, and Beck faced their leader, jaw clenching, clenching, clenching, her stomach right with it.

He was going to tell Kolinski.

More cold. She'd planned to come clean before taking the job officially at the end, but not now. It was *her* call to make, her *confession* to make.

"Is there a problem with you two?" Kolinski asked. "I thought this was sorted out."

"It *is* sorted out," Lauren said, shaking her head, and when she looked Beck in the eye again, his held through several thundering heartbeats, then he wordlessly climbed aboard the plane.

"You sure everything is sorted out?" Kolinski asked as he got on with checking her straps.

The answer was a lot more final in her head than it had been this morning when they'd been wrapped up in each other.

"I'm sure."

Sure it was over. He hadn't actually ratted her out, but it had been on the tip of his tongue. And that was his *starting* position? It had nowhere to go but worse.

Kolinski took her word, even if it was obviously another lie on her conscience, and she climbed onto the plane to find her place in line.

Lauren's jump and landing were flawless. Other, more experienced jumpers landed in trees, but not her. Beck had jumped just after her so he could make sure she went where she was supposed to go, and had followed her with one spin to land lengthways across the bare spot she'd aimed for.

He'd be proud if he wasn't presently angry at pretty much everyone. Himself for being irrational. Her for not listening, not even once. The fire, for being a fire.

Twenty minutes later, he had a shovel and a saw on his back, and moved with a group of five others—including Lauren—to where they were supposed to dig and cut. With simultaneous fires breaking out all over a national forest where people camped and hiked, they were spread as thinly as possible while still making any headway. By the time this was over, Beck feared the forest would look like it had been clear-cut.

Lauren started by climbing and sawing branches to bring the tree down clean, while he stayed on the ground and dug. With her up a tree, it was easier to keep track of her, but he was still aware of her every moment, despite it being complicated by the density of the smoke in the air and monitoring the comm for calls.

Less than full capability.

While digging, something hard bounded off his helmet. Small. Woody. Something thrown.

He looked up and found Lauren gesturing through a clearing in the trees.

What? he mouthed at her, the saws too loud to shout over.

Dog, she mouthed back.

Dog. Another damned dog.

And she was sending him after it?

They were close enough to the fire to see it

down the western slope and, sure enough, he saw black-and-white fur directly north.

It took only a moment to start moving. There was no way he wouldn't try to get the dog to come to him. He had rope. He'd tie it up, make it stay with them as they moved across the land.

He got halfway to it when the dog turned toward him and began to barrel in his direction at full speed.

Black-and-white. Kind of fluffy…

When it got to him, the breed became clear. Not a mutt. Purebred dog. Border collie. It barked and when he removed his glove and reached out to let it sniff, the dog snapped twice at his hand—biting, but not breaking the skin, just quick, near-frantic nips, then more barking. He ran back a short distance in the other direction.

"Beck!" Lauren's voice came through the din and he turned in time to see her running toward him, horror on her face. "It bit you!"

When she reached him, she grabbed his hand, looking for wounds.

"Not hard. He's agitated…"

She smoothed her fingers over the skin that was barely even pink, and looked over at the dog as he bound back.

Which was when he saw the tags and his stomach dropped through the earth.

Purebred with tags, alone in a national park, trying to get his attention.

"I think there's a family." He said the words as they came to him. "He's not here alone."

Beck knelt and the dog came running back. Before he got another bite in, Beck hooked his fingers under the collar so he could get a look at the tag.

"What's it say?"

"Henderson. Phone number."

"Crap."

"We knew there could be people out here."

"You think that's what this is? Lassie, Timmy's stuck in the well?"

He petted the dog, got nipped at again, and then let go so he could look at Lauren. "That's what I think."

"What do you want to do?"

"You know what I want to do."

She looked west, toward the fire, then the way the dog tried to lead them—northwest.

"There is another fire burning to the north. If the fire makes it past this break, we'll be stuck if we go that way," she said, and then reached for her comm to click it, and relayed the information, along with their decision to go.

Permission came unexpectedly fast. He wouldn't have even asked. And he didn't want to take her into an area where he wasn't already certain of their exit once they found the family, but he couldn't leave them there.

It was in him to apologize then, for what he'd almost done with Kolinski, but that would take time, and he didn't need to possibly make tensions even worse. No one needed to become more emotional in a deadly situation.

Later. Later he'd tell her he was sorry.

Lauren followed Beck and the dog at a near run up an incline steep enough she needed to use tree trunks to help haul herself up. There was no looking for a saner path up, not when they were following Lassie.

Never in her life would she have believed something like this could happen. It was like those stories people told about dolphins fighting off a shark to save a swimmer. Something that happened so rarely it might as well be an urban legend. And yet there they were, her burning lungs and limbs convincing her it was happening. The dog might not lead anywhere good, but they followed.

Through the trees, as they climbed higher, she began seeing disturbing amounts of orange glow cutting across the terrain in every direction, and mentally replayed updates they'd been given before heading out. Separate fires. All should be moving the same direction, but what she saw...

If her heart hadn't already been galloping, it would've rocketed up.

"Are you seeing four fires or three?" she asked, continuing to climb.

Beck couldn't stop and keep up with the dog, but he did look between the trees when he could, and opened the comm.

"This is Ellison. Want a fire check. Position. Size. Movement."

Did he usually call in? She knew from the day Treadwell had fallen and she'd spent so much time chasing Beck from one end of the field to the other that he didn't give updates.

Was he trying to change? She wished…

The suddenness of the change suggested otherwise, this was the kind of thing they'd been fighting about.

Report came in from the spotters quickly enough. Three fires, the one to the north large enough to wrap around the backside of a peak, appearing like a fourth, and the one they'd been tending had closed the gap behind them. Going back that way was no longer possible.

She stopped asking questions, he might think she was afraid.

She was, but letting him see that after the thing with Kolinski? Dumb. Once again, she was right back in that old pattern she'd had to operate in for years: hiding vulnerabilities from those she loved because they might use them against her.

There was nothing he could do to stop her from being on the mountain now, and he *had* included her in the decision to follow the dog, but she no longer trusted him. She might have won this time, but what would happen next time? This fire season was already one for the record books, and there would be a next time.

After she confessed, there would still probably be a lot more next times—the season was fierce and they needed the help. She might get a slap on the wrist for her application shenanigans, but if she confessed, that would help her case. If she could do the job, they'd keep her around. But Beck didn't want her doing it. He said *for now*, but she wasn't putting her life on hold to soothe him when he wouldn't get the help he needed to deal with his own problem.

Hell, at this point her application blunder was probably a lesser sin than her knowing Beck's issues and not reporting *him*. But *she* was loyal. Because despite knowing how this was going to go, and that it was over with them, she still wanted to see him whole. She didn't want anyone exposing her vulnerable spots, so how could she expose his?

They reached a rocky outcropping and the dog disappeared over it. Beck held out his hand to stop her going forward, and a moment later swung down himself.

"Sir?" His voice came from the other side, the one word the only confirmation Lauren needed to follow.

An unconscious man with a bloody leg lay on the ground, left femur protruding from his skin. The dog who'd led them there began a high, frantic whimper and lay down beside his human.

"Is he alive?" she asked, not able to see if the unconscious man's chest moved but noticing flies swarming the terrible wound, then the drag marks in the earth down the slope where he'd obviously scooted himself to reach the meager rock shelter.

Beck felt for a pulse, nodded to her. "Do you think he'll wake if I lift him? That break…"

"He's going to be in agony if you throw him over your shoulder," Lauren said, already pulling her pack off so she could fish out the collapsible stretcher that had been hers to carry.

"He might have to suffer it. If that direction isn't better…" he nodded down the other side from the one they'd traveled "…we can't carry him on a stretcher down the way we came up. It's too steep."

"Not if we go straight down, but we can cut across. Take it at a shallower angle."

"Fire's moving," he grunted, and then gestured

for the stretcher, which she handed over for him to begin assembling.

"That bone is bad. I know it's already been exposed to the elements, and worse, but we should at least try to cover it," she said, getting the man's pulse and directing, "Call in. Tell them we found Henderson."

"Henderson?"

"The name on the tags," she explained, then let go of his wrist. "His heart is going too fast. And he feels hot. Do you have an unopened water bottle?"

She knew enough about first aid to know compound fractures became infected very easily, and he'd been there at least the night. The storm that sparked the fires hadn't dropped as much rain as it had lightning, but it had wet the ground so his dry clothes had become caked along the sides with mud when he'd slid under the ledge.

"Yeah, why?"

"I don't know. I just…feel like I should at least pour the water over the end and rinse the…" She wasn't going to say it. She didn't actually even want to think what bugs were in the wound.

"Sorry I don't have salt, seems like saline would be better for flushing any wounds."

"It would."

He laid the stretcher out, then pulled his pack off to dig out the water and first-aid supplies.

"Here. Gauze and bandages. Wrap it, anything is better than nothing."

She took the supplies and began opening them while looking for some way to wrap the leg. He was out. They might be able to give his leg the kind of jerk that would pull the bone back into the skin, but that could make things worse. Drag infection directly into the body.

She laid the large gauze pad over the raw end of the bone, then lifted his leg enough to wrap the elastic bandage around and around, just to cover. Keep the bugs away…

"Should we rouse him?"

"Pain will be unbearable," Beck said, finally raising base on the comm.

Treadwell responded as Beck relayed the situation and their location, got directions where to go—down to the river. Follow it out. An ambulance would be waiting. And there they'd part. It might be possible for her to work with him out here, but continuing to do so for the rest of camp would be torturing herself for no reason.

"What about bracing his neck?"

Beck looked at the man, then shook his head. "He scooted himself up the mountain. His head seems well attached. Besides, I don't have a neck brace in there. And we need to move, the wind is kicking up. Everything's going to spread faster."

Right. Stay focused on what was before them.

Injured man. Fast-moving fire. Treacherous mountainous terrain.

"Okay, I'll get his head until we clear the ledge, then we swap."

He looked at her strangely.

"Head's heavier, but the ledge wants someone short. Might as well use our advantages." They had a few of them, and even if a future together couldn't happen, they could use their advantages today.

Halfway down the mountain, Lauren could just make out something large and white on the riverbank. "Beck? I think there's a boat…"

"God, I hope so."

This trek was already worse than the pack carry, but at least it came with built-in reward. He might survive. And the dog…

As they hurried, and sometimes slid, Beck checked in for updates. All smokejumpers were rigged with GPS to make them easier to find if things got hairy, but he still did it. Small victory, but she'd take it.

CHAPTER THIRTEEN

A TWO-MILE TREK became a three-hour endurance test.

Beck had to fight every urge in him to put the unconscious man over his shoulder and abandon the stretcher, just so they could move faster. It wasn't that Lauren wasn't pulling her weight, but moving over taxing terrain was hard enough without carrying a stretcher and dodging a worried dog perpetually underfoot.

By the time they reached the water, it should've become easier, and would've been except for a stretch of narrow ledge they had to pass to reach the boat without climbing over another steep rise.

"What do you want to do?" She stopped and looked back at him, then pointedly over his shoulder to the burning hillside acres away behind them. She carried the handles of the stretcher at each hip so she could move forward instead of miles of dangerous backing. They didn't have time for anything that slowed them down.

"We don't have a choice." He nodded to the handles. "We might need to change the way we're carrying if you can't walk with your arms at the sides."

The sound of rushing water made the decision even more treacherous. It looked deep, and violent. Even if it were only deep enough to come to her ribs, it still moved with the kind of strength that would make it impossible to walk and carry the man—who'd yet to awaken.

"Cross that bridge when we come to it," she muttered, and then started walking. The warnings in his belly hit earsplitting decibels, but there was nothing else. Nothing but the fire behind them and the water beside him. Nothing but remembering his mother's terrible decision. As they walked, it was right there at the front of his mind, taking the attention he should've been paying to his feet and the path. He'd slid twice and nearly dropped the man or knocked Lauren into the water by the time they reached the end.

"Give me a second, I have to wipe my hands… palms…sweating…" she panted, moving to a spot where she could bend to put her end down. Which was when she looked past him to the narrow strip of precarious land they'd just traveled. "Where's the dog?"

The dog?

He turned as well. The border collie that had

led them to his injured owner was nowhere in sight.

"Damn," he muttered, and then held up one hand. "I'll go grab him, if I can."

A quick look back at the water offered no comfort to him. If the dog had fallen in, it would've probably been swept past before he'd known to look.

And the fire.

Running back toward the fire... He swallowed the bitter plug in his throat. It wasn't that far, not even half a football field. It was the bend in the ledge that made it impossible to see the other end.

"Be careful. Yell if you have trouble."

"If I have trouble, you grab the handles of that stretcher and drag it to the water," he said, pointing to another outcropping with a far wider ledge. "The boat is just past that bend, if I remember right. You can make that with him if I don't come back."

Her eyes narrowed, and she folded her arms. Staying there to argue wouldn't serve any purpose. She'd move when the fire came, if he didn't come back. She wasn't suicidal.

Moving faster than the first time across, he'd reached the other end in minutes and found the dog pacing back and forth, whining as he looked at the ground then at the water.

"Come on, buddy. It's okay." He didn't feel like

talking sweet, but flies and honey... If the dog ran now, he'd have to leave it behind. The very idea of that made his stomach lurch. He might have vomited on the spot if there had been anything inside him after a long day.

A little whistle, crouching, hand outstretched... When the fluffy black-and-white dog came to him, Beck snatched him up from the ground and turned to head back down the path.

Immediately, he knew he'd screwed up, holding the dog to face the water that scared him.

It took all his balance and strength to keep hold of the suddenly thrashing animal. About halfway there, the dog whipped his upper body hard to one side, knocking his head against Beck's temple. His head ringing, he became aware of gravity shifting below him. Tilting. Falling...

No hands to grab with. No land behind to step on. He heaved the loudly yelping dog toward the ground as he fell back.

There was cold, then pain, then nothing.

A terrible yelp sounded from up the path, and by the time Lauren straightened from the crouch where she'd been checking the unconscious man's pulse the dog came rocketing toward her, tail and hind end tucked down in fear.

Where was Beck?

"Beck!" She shouted his name, but caught sight

of something orange bobbing in the water, and her heart slammed into overdrive.

Due to the nature of the water, he didn't rush in one direction but bounced like a pinball in the rocky, whirlpool-laden waters. As quickly as she could, Lauren scrambled onto the biggest, deepest rocky bend and held on with one hand while stretching as hard as she could over the water.

Two more hits, she couldn't even tell what part of him was hitting the rocks, just that he wasn't moving on his own. His head wasn't coming up but stayed in the water.

Any second, come on... He'd be there. She could grab him. Get him out somehow.

A sudden rush of the water nearly shot him right past her. Her fingers slid over the heavy heat-resistant material of his pants and jacket, only finding purchase at his collar.

"Beck!" She shouted his name again, jerking with all her might to try and get him out of the water, but the suit had filled, making him heavier.

She managed to lift his head out of the water and tugged him a little closer. "Come on, wake up. Wake up!"

He coughed, the first sign of life she'd heard, and she almost choked on tears springing to her eyes.

Alive. But not awake.

Bracing her foot on a closer, slippery boulder,

she got enough leverage to drag his shoulders up the rock and did the only thing she could think of—let go with her other handhold long enough to slap him before the water jerked them both in.

On the second slap, he coughed again and began to flail. It took her screaming his name more times than she could count before he roused enough to find purchase on the rocks and help her pull him out.

Red water ran down the side of his face from his dark hair. His nose was also clearly never going to be the same. She almost regretted slapping him.

"Can you stand up?"

He coughed more, then looked in the direction they'd come from, and the even closer fire.

No direct answer, he just accepted her hands in assistance and staggered to his feet.

The protective gear he wore weighed him down, and he began stripping out of it. "Go."

"Not without you."

"Drag him to the boat. I'll come. Don't come back. Go." He breathed hard and fast, and even with the water rushing she could hear wet sounds in his rasping breaths.

Disobedient as she was, she didn't start moving until she'd helped him out of the pants, leaving him in sodden shorts, T-shirt, and boots.

"Go," he said again, and since she couldn't help them both at once, Lauren did.

They weren't far from the boat, Beck had said, but she wasn't sure how far, only knew she had to get there.

As she dragged the stretcher, it began to come apart. Forty or fifty yards to a short stretch of pebbled shore where a motorboat had been pulled onto the shore. She dragged the now canvas sled and man there to find the dog waiting.

Wasting no time, she heaved the man into the boat, as careful as she could be of his leg, given the situation, coaxed the skittish dog in as well, then ran back for Beck.

She'd never felt fear like the thousand icy needles down her back. His head had to have hit hard to make it bleed like that, didn't it? Was he even still up and walking? Breathing? He'd breathed in water, and with those rocks he'd probably broken ribs.

She almost ran smack into him as she got around a bend, and ducked under his arm, spun, and slung an arm around his waist to give him something to lean on.

"I said…" he started. But when he looked into her eyes, and the tears she could do nothing to stop, whatever he'd been about to say died in his throat.

There was no time to explore it, no time to

reflect. No time to let him rest, even if it felt cruel to make him continue. She could feel the heat from the fire now as it moved fast over dry brush. They needed to get to the boat, get the boat into the water, and figure out how to make it go—the one part of this she had no idea how to do, or even if he'd still be conscious by the time they got there.

"If you think I'm going to leave you here, you're too stupid to do this job." The hiccup that came from her at the end of her half-shouted words surprised them both.

Something like horror shrouded his dark eyes, an expression she knew she mirrored in the face of bright, red blood running more thickly now down his cheek.

"Shut up," she shouted, although he hadn't said anything, and sped up, making him walk faster than she knew he should be.

Every step pained him, she heard it in his breathing and the occasional gasp when she squeezed a little tighter to keep him upright—it seemed he was always about to fall over.

It felt like it took a year to make it to the boat, and there was a brief argument about him wanting to help push it into the water—as if he could—and she finally got them in.

"I don't know what to do."

"Motor," he said, then took a ragged breath. "Works like a lawnmower."

"Okay."

"Pull the cord." He gave the steps, with several pauses. Ending with, "Don't go fast."

Right. Because if she crashed them into something, the water would get them, not the fire.

The river became wider and more shallow dozens of yards downriver, and as it broadened out, it became less fast-moving.

"Your comm working?" Beck was still with it enough to keep her focused, prompting her to call in once the way got smoother.

Treadwell answered, and she asked for two ambulances and followed his instructions on where to take the boat. Through the miracle of GPS, he'd been monitoring their progress and was ready for them.

It wasn't far or long. A couple of miles of awkward boating until they reached a bridge where two ambulances sat, lights on, doors open, EMT teams and police on the shore with stretchers, ready to pull them in.

Beck didn't put up a fight about being strapped onto the stretcher, and if she hadn't been worried before, she would've been then.

He'd gone quite pale, whiteness around his mouth speaking of the pain she knew he was in, and maybe reduced lung capacity—his breathing sounded so bad.

She and Treadwell climbed into the ambulance with him. The police took custody of the heroic border collie, and the other ambulance took the still-unconscious Henderson.

"What happened out there?" Treadwell asked *her*, and she wasn't entirely sure, but filled in what she knew. Beck had gone back for the dog, something had happened, he'd fallen. She'd fished him out.

The report didn't take long, and the only reason she knew Beck wasn't unconscious or asleep was the whiteness of his knuckles where he gripped the sheet.

Decisions that had been brewing in her mind came to a head all at once.

It wasn't because he hadn't wanted her to go today, or because she felt any confusion about where she belonged—whatever questions she'd had were answered. But she wanted to do this right, out in the open. Before she lost her nerve she said, "Chief, I need to tell you something."

Beck's eyes whipped open, skewering her over the short distance to where she perched at the foot of his stretcher. The chief opposite her watched her with equal attention. She turned her gaze back to the man in control of her career, focusing there.

"Before the first jump this season, I had never actually finished my skydiving training…"

CHAPTER FOURTEEN

DESPITE NOT KNOWING whether she'd be allowed at the camp come Monday, Lauren had the good fortune of being in for now and given the honor of a four a.m. ride the next morning by a local policeman Treadwell called in.

She'd been looked over immediately upon arriving, deemed perfectly fine aside from some dehydration, and released before nightfall. Beck hadn't been so lucky. His injuries required admittance in the hours in between. Treadwell had been kind enough to bring her updates about his condition after finding her loitering in the hallway outside his room, unable to go inside.

Concussion.

Fractured ribs.

Water in his lungs he hadn't been able to cough out and they were forcing him to now.

Prognosis: he'd live.

But he was out for the season.

Now, at five in the morning, she soaked in the

tub, waiting for the sun to come up so she could call her father.

She'd made decisions over the long hours in the waiting room to learn Beck's condition, and even without knowing whether or not she'd be welcome at camp come Monday, she knew she wouldn't be returning to her family's station in San Francisco. She wanted to tell him that. Tell him everything, actually. Not to gloat, she didn't have that in her, even if she now knew beyond any doubt she was doing what she was meant to.

It was just time. Get her life in order. Make hard decisions. The only thing she could control was living her life without fear of what other people would say. Whatever Dad said didn't matter as long as she was satisfied with herself.

She couldn't pick her family. She loved them, and had to figure out how to deal with them and have a relationship.

But with Beck? They hadn't exactly talked about what they were going to do after camp, but she'd hoped there would be an after. Now all she could think was that she couldn't stay with a man who either held her back or had a death wish.

Death wish might not be fair. He *had* been trying to survive, walking to her through the pain that made him move at a slow stagger, the head injuries messing with his balance… He hadn't said so, would never say so, but he'd been *trying* to reach the boat.

Death wish wasn't a fair label. Martyr might be.

Someone who wanted his death to mean something?

Someone who wanted his *life* to mean something?

When the bath started growing cold, she climbed out, pulled on a robe, and went to get her phone.

Her father answered on the first ring, and in a tone so calm she even surprised herself, Lauren laid it all out for him. Her harrowing day. Her lie. Her possibly being fired before she was actually hired. The man they'd saved. That she wouldn't be returning home to work again.

"So, you're asking me to help you transfer to another house?"

"No, Dad. I'm not asking you for anything," she said, and then the thought occurred… "Actually, there is something you can do for me if you're willing."

"What?"

"My friend? His mom died and was swept away by the river near their house up here about fifteen years ago. Never found her that he knows of. If I can get you his DNA, do you think you can get one of your cop buddies to run it against any Jane Does they've found in the past fifteen years?"

"How are you going to get his DNA?"

"His toothbrush is here."

"Don't know if it'll fly, legally, but for another member of the service I'll ask. I know some people."

Of course he did. Chief Richard Autry knew everyone. "Thanks, Dad."

"You let me know where you land, sugar bean."

Her lower lip wobbled, but she managed to say, "I will. Love you."

She hung up before the tears really started to pour.

The smell of antiseptic was as far from a forest as possible, and made every second he was forced to spend in the hospital suck.

What made it worse was Lauren not being there. He couldn't believe he'd grown so hooked on her presence in such a short period of time. And he didn't want to believe what her absence probably meant.

Treadwell, currently sleeping in the recliner beside Beck's bed, had kept him awake for the first twenty-four hours by playing cards, making him do crosswords, play along with game shows when he found them on TV, narrated a fishing show in such a fashion that no one could sleep through it, and refused to listen when Beck told him for the thousandth time to go home.

"Here for vitals," a woman in scrubs announced when she came in, waking Treadwell.

Beck stuck out his arm.

"Is he getting out today?" the chief asked.

Beck grunted, "You're getting out today."

"Briefly, maybe."

"Have to wait for the doctor to come by, but probably not. Want to make sure his lungs have recovered enough to be let loose in the wild," the nurse said, then gave him an encouraging smile that did nothing to encourage him. "You're one of the smokejumpers who brought in Mr. Henderson, right?"

"Yeah." Beck wanted to hear about Lauren, but Treadwell had refused to talk about her any of the times he'd asked. Hearing about Henderson was the next best thing. "How's he doing?"

Her smile widened and she wrote down Beck's vitals as she took them. "He's awake."

"Yeah?"

"Yeah. They're taking good care of him."

"Good news," Treadwell said softly from the recliner. "You and Autry made a good team."

Made.

Past tense.

Beck's stomach churned, but he held his tongue until the nurse was done prodding him.

He wanted to contradict the chief, *make a good team*, but she might no longer be willing to put up with him.

When they were alone, he asked, "Are you talking about her now?"

"You're better."

Well enough to hear bad news. "Have you talked to her?"

"On all my trips out of your rooms until the wee hours."

"She's all right?"

"She's uninjured. Don't know about *all right*."

Of course she wasn't completely all right. He knew he'd scared her. He just hadn't really been able to consider how much until she'd come back for him, and pushed him along through her own tears. Lauren crying… Finally giving in to the tears she usually contained. The idea slammed him in the guts every time.

"Does she get to keep her job?" he asked, because he couldn't not ask.

Treadwell waited for him to look over and nodded. "She does. I let her know last night, but I'm busting her back to pure rookie status. No more jumps until training is over, and I'm making her lead a talk about what you two went through today."

"But you know she can do it, she doesn't need to go back a step."

"I know she can do it. Just like I knew you didn't need to go through the training to do your job. But it still helped you."

"I'm not so sure."

"Why not?"

Beck could tell him the truth. Tell him everything, the things he didn't talk about to anyone but Lauren. The things she'd said Treadwell deserved to know. But he might think the training had had a less positive impact on Beck than he'd thought.

"Are you glad she told you? We'd already remedied the situation."

"I need my people to trust I'll have their backs when the situation arises, that I'll make the right call for them and everyone else."

Treadwell couldn't have made a more loaded statement if he'd spent the whole night crafting and polishing the words.

Whether or not Treadwell knew that Beck still struggled with that, Beck knew.

She'd been brave. Her telling the chief the truth was a much bigger risk than him telling the chief now.

It wasn't so much that he wanted to hide these things, it was just hard to think about, to talk about. And there was something to be said for avoiding pity…

But he didn't want to be the mess he'd become.

He wanted to be better. Be someone deserving of Lauren, not some pale shadow of her bravery.

Even if he'd already screwed up too badly to ever get her back, he could follow her example.

"Will you go home and get some sleep if I tell you what's been going on with me?" As the words came, Beck had already started shaking his head at himself. "I don't want you having another heart attack from the antiseptic stench and lousy food."

Lauren opened the door of the cabin after a long day, and stumbled over the single step up.

Beck sat on the sofa, calmly watching her.

Something gave her the power to grab the doorframe and stop herself going down at the last second and avoid eating floor.

"Hey…" she greeted him, as if it hadn't been nine days since she'd seen him.

"Hey," he said quietly in return, sitting forward slowly on the sofa. "I hope it's all right for me to come in while you're out. I realize it's not exactly my cabin anymore."

"It's fine. I mean, your stuff is still here." She swept her arm toward the bedroom he'd occupied, and saw it standing open with a stuffed duffel bag acting as a doorstop.

He probably shouldn't be carrying that. Broken ribs didn't heal overnight, and it only felt like forever since he'd been smashed along the river. "You should let me carry that for you."

"Yeah, maybe." He reached out and tapped a mason jar full of salts on the table before him. "Thought you could probably use another batch, and now I see you, I know you can. You look wiped out."

"I've been doing extra PT."

"Why?"

"To make sure I'm as strong as I can be," she lied. Funny how easy it was to fall back into patterns to cover those vulnerable spots. She'd sworn off them and proclaimed she was going to live in the open air, but with Beck... "Actually, I've been doing extra every day so that I sleep well."

"Why aren't you sleeping well?"

"I'm sleeping okay. I just want to be extra tired so I'll go right to sleep."

His gaze sharpened, and she noticed how dark he was beneath his eyes, a shadow deeper than simple sleepless nights.

"Are both of your eyes black?"

"Smashing into rocks with my head did it." He gestured to the place on the side where she remembered him bleeding. "Treadwell said it knocked some sense into me. I'm not sure it was the rocks."

"Did something else hit you?"

"Just you. Like a fire truck."

The imagery was so mixed she didn't know whether it was meant to be good or not. Hitting like a truck didn't sound good; knocking sense into him did...

"I'm pretty sure I didn't."

"You did," he said so softly she wouldn't have been sure she'd heard it if she hadn't been watching his mouth form the words. "Why do you want to go right to sleep? Don't want to lie there thinking about how badly I screwed up?"

Assigning blame to their catastrophe felt like a betrayal. He'd screwed up, she'd screwed up. They were both screwed up. "Don't want to dwell on what could've been. I guess."

Her throat tightened as she spoke, until the end when her voice cracked, unable to contain the emotion, even without looking at him and the sadness she knew she'd see.

It was enough to get her moving again, straight past the sofa into the little kitchenette where she'd stashed a cooler and drinks.

Her hands shook hard enough that the wet plastic bottle of electrolyte-imbued drink shot from her fingers, bounced between her feet, and ricocheted backward across the kitchen floor before she'd even touched the lid.

It rolled over the linoleum, then suddenly stopped.

When she turned around, Beck had picked up the bottle and now wiped down the wet exterior on the comfortable-looking gray T-shirt he wore, then opened it for her.

It looked like an overture, him holding the drink out to her in invitation, but all she could do was stare at it, and then past to the dark, worried eyes of the man she spent every minute thinking about.

"If you take the drink, you're not obligated to take me back, you know," he said softly, plucking the thoughts straight from her mind.

Not obligated to *take me back*.

Did that mean he wanted her back? God knew, she wanted him, but her self-esteem had become progressively stronger over the past week. Wanting something and being able to have it weren't the same thing. Wanting something didn't make it good for her.

Snarky responses were her emotional currency. She was good at them and other tactics that kept her apart from others. Kept her safe. But standing there, her mouth dry and her eyes damp, she couldn't think of anything to say.

Drinking the drink would at least keep her mouth busy, less pressure to say something.

She took the bottle and drank deeply until about a third of it was gone.

All under the weight of his sad gaze.

"I don't know what to say. If you want to say something, just—"

"I talked to Treadwell," he cut in, skipping over the relationship talk into something safer.

Something he'd know she wanted to hear, she'd been pressing him to do it. A safe subject.

"What did you tell him?"

"Everything," he said, not quite a whisper but the kind of soft talk that wanted closeness. To be closer than they were, standing across the tiny kitchenette from one another.

"What's everything?"

"What happened to my mom. Why I lost the thread of what I was doing last season. Why I'm still struggling to get my feet under me."

No ring of finality came with his words, they almost sounded like a question.

"What changed your mind?"

"He wouldn't leave." Beck chuckled a little. "Slept by my bed, couldn't get rid of him. Wore me down, I guess."

Ah. Nothing to do with their trip down the mountain. Or her.

"I'm glad he stayed. So he kept asking?"

"No. I asked him if he was going to let you stay." He watched her too closely, as if also afraid of putting a foot out of line. Was this him trying to salvage a friendship? A working relationship? Something more? "He said he'd already talked to you about it, and you were staying. He was glad you told him because he needs his people to know he'll have their backs."

"Oh." She could see how that would be motivating. Not something to feel disappointment over. "I do feel that way. I guess he just needed to absorb it a bit, and in the ambulance, it was kind of a lot to take in while your condition was obviously the biggest concern. I probably should've waited, but once I'd decided…"

"When did you decide?"

She shifted, the urge to conceal again proving to her how far she still had to go to live in the open air. Not so much because the answer would hurt her this time, but it might hurt him. It definitely was a much closer blow to the subject they weren't talking about.

"In the hangar," she said finally, then drew a deep breath to fortify herself. "Treadwell has said he would welcome me onto his team after camp. But I told him I needed to talk to you first. It's your team too…"

"I want you there," he said without hesitation. "I want you there even if you won't take me back today. Not because I want to keep an eye on you but because I'm hoping that eventually I'll prove myself to you, that I'll be able to get myself out of the red."

"Beck…"

"Because I love you. I knew it that morning, before we left. I can't excuse what I came damned close to doing, but I need to explain to you how I actually got there and said I loved you the first time in that way. I know how dirty that was. I know you probably don't even believe it…"

"I believe it." She waved a hand. "Slow down. For a man who never talks, you're saying a lot of things. I think I may have gotten used to listening slower."

He grinned then, and before she knew it he stood before her and had her cheeks in his hands, his lips pressing softly to her forehead.

"That's not slower," she choked, eyes stinging and ears suddenly itching, because that's just how lucky she was—every time she cried, she wanted to sit on the floor and kick her ear like a dog.

"Sorry. Sorry…" He reached up to scratch his head, seemed to remember the wound, and pulled his hand away again. "I don't remember what I was saying."

"You were saying you were a jerk to say you loved me to manipulate me not to jump."

"Wasn't manipulation," he argued. "It was pleading. Here's…here's the thing. On your first jump, when I went without you and then got to the ground to see your chute in the air, heading for the fire, the possibility of all the things that could happen to you became some kind of gruesome certainty they *would*. The more I felt for you, the bigger those ideas became in my mind. I know it's not fair. I know it's not rational. I know… Actually, I have a standing appointment with the counselor to try and screw my head on straight. I'm talking to her, and all I really want to do is talk to *you*."

Getting help, that was something real. Telling Treadwell. Talking to her without her having to badger and push.

"Or touch you. Which… I'm going to put my hands in my pockets to avoid."

It was cute. The man who glowered his way through life actually looked like he was about ten years younger as he stood there, hands stretching the pockets of his jeans down from how far in he'd shoved them.

"You're not angry that I didn't come visit?"

"I know why you didn't come, honey. But I want you to know, it wasn't your absence that changed my mind about what I've been doing."

"The chief?"

"It was your tears," he said, his hands jerking the pockets again, controlling that urge to touch and connect. "Seeing the misery and fear on your face. Something you said back on the bus that day about what if my mom had been the one to survive. I saw it in your eyes when you came back for me."

Her breathing sped up and her vision began to wave like rising heat. She was going to cry again. If she opened her mouth to talk, what came out wouldn't be words.

"I never want you to have to live with what I've lived with."

She gave up trying to make words take shape in her head and just held her hand out to him. Both of his shot from his pockets at once and he pulled her close, grunting a little from how hard he'd tugged and she'd impacted.

That got through.

"Your ribs!" She registered that her voice had gone screeching into the stratosphere, but he didn't let go of her even when she made to pull back.

"I have a fresh batch of salts," he whispered into her hair, and she gave in and rested her forehead against the center of his chest, her hands on his hips because she still couldn't bring herself to squeeze back as the tears began to fall and her nose stopped working.

The last sniff she managed through her rapidly swelling sinuses confirmed he still had the smell of hospital on him.

"You do seem to need a bath," she teased, tilting her head back to look at him. "But I do too."

"Honey and dirt." He looked at her mouth long and hard. "I'm about to ask you to have a bath with me while still wondering if it's okay to kiss you… See how much I have to learn about relationships?"

She lifted her mouth, not warning him about how salty she probably was. Or that her nose might be about to run and he should kiss her quickly. When his lips pressed to hers, trembling met trembling, regret and relief, and a golden ray of hope, warming like morning's first sunshine. Bright. So full of promise as to be blinding.

When he lifted his head, his gaze traveled over her wet cheeks and he lifted his hands to brush the tears away. "You're still crying."

"I've been working myself to exhaustion to avoid it." She laughed a little. "But it's easing up. We could have a bath, and then the wetness won't be so obvious."

His smile was all cheek as he turned with her to walk to the table to fetch the salts to take with them. "You have good ideas."

"Sometimes," she said, feeling the first urge to smile in forever, and with an uncontrollable urge to tease him, to play. "I hope you don't think we're going to have sex in here. You're hurt. You don't need jostling."

"You planning to jostle me?"

"Nothing strenuous. Like that bag. You can't carry that bag right now. Were you going to take it to your truck?"

He stopped at the bathroom door, still holding her hand, still looking a little worried. "If you're not ready."

"Really?" she asked, rising on her toes to kiss him. "There you go again, thinking I can't handle what I say I can handle."

EPILOGUE

Two years and three months later...

LAUREN ELLISON STOOD at the kitchen window to the newly rebuilt wooded cottage she shared with her husband, staring out at the shiny new workshop he'd disappeared into. It had been almost two hours since they'd returned home from his mother's long-overdue memorial service.

California's records had provided no matches for Beck's DNA, but two months ago officials in southern Oregon had contacted them. Scant remains washed ashore years ago had finally been tested. They'd found her. Proof she'd drowned, not burned. A few weeks' bureaucratic wrangling and they'd finally obtained the permission required to bring Molly Ellison home.

He'd seemed all right after the quiet service, surrounded by his new family, people who'd never met his mother but who wanted to pay their respects to the woman who'd given the Autry clan its fourth son. It had been two hours, alone in the one place on their little homestead she'd promised not to go.

They'd reached that unbelievable place where anything could be said as long as it was said with love. At work. At home. Anywhere. Best friends. Partners. Lovers. And, someday soon, parents.

Actually, he was in the one place she'd promised not to go *inside*. She could go to the door. Just to check on him. Make sure he knew she was there if he needed her.

She hurried out the back door and soon stood at the door of the man cave, and knocked. "Babe? You still in there?"

In seconds, he appeared there, still looking crisp in the white button-down he'd worn to the service. Not falling apart. Not bereft, although she still saw the sadness of the day lingering in his inky eyes.

"I'm not going anywhere."

He leaned down to steal a little kiss, and since it seemed final, she nodded and made to step back from the door.

"Just needed to make sure you were okay." She still wasn't sure he was, but the hand at her waist firmed and began to steer her around so she stood with her back to the door. "Um...if you want me to go..."

"I don't." He stayed with her outside the building, and when she looked over her shoulder at him, he smiled. "I have a surprise in the workshop. But I want you to close your eyes. It's not wrapped."

He wanted her to come inside his hideaway? She'd spent months wondering what he was making out here—chairs, tables, a fancy hutch for the metric boatload of papercraft supplies she'd accumulated after realizing last winter she had time to put together scrapbooks of their exploits for their future children.

"Is it furniture? People don't wrap furniture, do they?" He'd brought in wood and supplies the day the small building had been considered functional. The woodshop was his second favorite place to be, outside the woods. Or maybe third, if bed with her got counted as a prime location, and it did. "It's big, right?"

"Play along." He put one large, warm hand over her eyes, then wrapped his other arm around her waist to spin her slowly back toward the building, using his body to propel her forward. "Step."

She did, trusting him to steer her but still reaching out ahead of her with waving hands to keep from hitting anything.

Not ten paces in, he stopped them, pulling her back against his warmth and breathing in her ear. "You ready?"

"Uh…*yeah*! You know I'm not good at playing along or playing it cool." She wrapped her hands around the hand covering her eyes and gave a little tug.

His hand dropped and with the low lighting inside it took her eyes time to adjust.

Darkness began to fade and lines appeared, then shapes, and finally detail.

Arcs for feet, legs, wooden spindles, a mattress. And a teddy bear in the center. Cradle. Rocking cradle. For the children they didn't yet have and hadn't actually started to plan yet.

She felt herself moving forward again, and he let go so she could touch it. Running her fingers over the smooth, polished wood still didn't make it seem real. "This is what you've been making all this time?"

"Don't like it?" he asked. "I thought…make the cradle and then, when I was ready, I'd give it to you."

Ready? Did ready mean…?

"When did you get done?"

"This morning."

She couldn't stop touching the smooth, cool gray wood. "What kind of wood is this?"

"Tan oak." He answered all the questions except the one she hadn't asked. She never wanted to push when it came to children, but this… She had to ask.

"So, this morning you got finished and you're just really excited and want to show me?"

"This morning I got finished, and realized as soon as I placed the bear in it that I was ready."

"You're ready?" she repeated, and left the beautiful, still-rocking cradle to return to her even more beautiful husband. "Are you trying to tell me you've gone and gotten yourself in the family way, Mr. Ellison?"

He smiled at her teasing and pulled his arms around her as she pressed close. "I'm willing to try. We can just have lots of unprotected sex and whoever gets pregnant first can do the heavy lifting on this one."

"That's good to know, because I have something to tell you." She tilted her head back to watch his face, to experience every drop of joy this life had to offer. "I win."

* * * * *

If you enjoyed this story, check out these other great reads from Amalie Berlin

Healed Under the Mistletoe
Their Christmas to Remember
Back in Dr. Xenakis' Arms
The Rescue Doc's Christmas Miracle

All available now!